THE MIAMI BRIGADE

THE MIAMI BRIGADE

BY

NICK FATTOR

INKWATER
PRESS

PORTLAND • OREGON
INKWATERPRESS.COM

Publisher: Inkwater Press | www.inkwaterpress.com

ISBN-13 978-1-62901-689-4 | ISBN-10 1-62901-689-6

1 3 5 7 9 10 8 6 4 2

CONTENTS

ACKNOWLEDGEMENTS

1.) My Father
To my dad who encouraged me to write for years and who has been a good father. We have been through the storm and found a safe harbor at last.

2.) My ECU History Professors
To my ECU professors who kept my attention and are some of the best educators I have ever met. Godspeed in your lives gentlemen as the world needs more like you.
Dr. Clampitt, Dr. Bean, Dr. Cowger, Dr. Sutton and Dr. Mount

3.) My Audience
To those who bought this book I express my thanks as the Bay of Pigs Invasion was an event that led directly to the Cuban Missile Crisis. It was one of the boldest plans of the CIA and had it been successful all of Cuba would have been changed by the outcome. Despite all the good intentions of the CIA they did not prepare for any of the worst case scenarios and instead forged ahead with a misguided plan that was doomed to failure.

INTRODUCTION

ON JANUARY 2, 1959 CASTRO ASSUMED POWER IN CUBA. BATISTA was gone and after a struggle which lasted over five years Communism ruled on an island only 90 miles from the United States. Since 1898 when America first got involved with Cuba the island had been guided by its powerful neighbor to the north. Batista was corrupt and ruthless, but he was liked by American politicians as he supported capitalism and its many vices. Fidel Castro by comparison ended the cozy relationship with the United States that Batista had enjoyed for years.

Communism was the new law of the land in Cuba in 1959 and it was no friend to America. Naturally the CIA was dismayed by events that were taking place in Cuba. Since their creation in 1947 the CIA had dedicated themselves to ensuring that Communism was combated anywhere it arose. With Cuba only 90 miles from the coast of the United States action was deemed necessary. A hasty plan was assembled and modified over late 1960 as the CIA laid out an invasion proposal that was as bold as it was lacking in military realities.

With Castro in power and employing brutality there were also people who wanted to rid Cuba of the dictator and return its government to a non-Communist form. These Cuban exiles lived in Miami, Florida as it was the closest major US city to

Havana. In late 1960 just after John F. Kennedy was elected president a military plan was presented to President Eisenhower. Despite his strong distaste for Castro's regime, Eisenhower had less than three months in office. Launching a major military operation with such little time in power was not a wise political move. On January 20, 1961 Eisenhower informed Kennedy of the plan to remove Castro from power. It was bold, risky and not without its flaws, but the plan was available if Kennedy decided to take action against Castro.

John F. Kennedy was a president that believed in the United States being a force for good in the world to counter the Soviet Union and Communism. He viewed Castro as a problem that had to be dealt with in a quick fashion. On April 17, 1961 the Bay of Pigs Invasion was launched in Cuba with a force of 1,400 Cubans exiles being landed before they encountered strong resistance. For the next three days the Cuban exiles fought for their very lives as 114 were killed and the rest were compelled to surrender on April 20. The brigade's supplies were gone and they faced total annihilation. In mid-December 1962 the Cuban exiles were returned to the United States in exchange for 43 million dollars in US Aid which was given to Cuba.

In retrospect the Bay of Pigs Invasion was a military plan that had no chance of success as the forces arrayed against the 1,400 Cuban exiles were too much to overcome. The leaders of the CIA had come up with a plan that lacked reality testing as any lieutenant in the US Army could have explained that failure was going to be the result. President Kennedy served with distinction and valor during World War II as a PT Boat commander in the US Navy. However he had placed too much faith in the advice he was given by the CIA.

It was the CIA senior officials that strongly pushed for the Bay of Pigs Invasion as they believed getting rid of Castro was possible. All of the CIA plans were based wishful thinking instead of military realities and facts. Castro was advised by Che Guevara to create militias shortly before April 1961. The end result was that Cuba was ready to counter a shoestring invasion launched by the United States. This was not the D-Day

Invasion or anything close to it. A handful of A-26 attack planes were used and nearly all of them were shot down during the invasion. The invasion force was under trained and over eager the men who reached the beach were fighting without naval or air support for the better part of three days in addition to losing over half of their supplies.

GOODBYE BATISTA

PRESIDENT BATISTA WAS AWOKEN FROM HIS SLEEP BY THE SOUND OF gunfire and artillery shells in the distance. His wife Marta also heard the very disturbing noises and got dressed along with her husband in a rapid manner from their current outfit of pajamas. Colonel Juan Alverez entered the bedroom and informed Batista that it was no longer safe for him to stay in Havana. For seven long years a guerrilla war against Batista had been raging. Castro was one of many men who wanted Batista gone.

The forces loyal to Batista had used brutal measures to crush the rebellion, but were unable to stop the slow and steady progress of Castro. The time had finally come to flee as Batista could not rely on his men to protect him. In addition the people would not rise up and rally behind their leader. Batista was brutal and corrupt which limited his supporters to a small band of wealthy citizens willing to tolerate him. The Cuban Army had proven unable to defeat the guerrillas led by Castro.

Col. Alverez was eager for Batista and his family to head to the Havana Airport as there was only one safe way for them to leave Cuba, by plane. A Cuban Airlines DC-7 sat waiting for the Batista family as this plane was reserved for their use only. Alverez knew that the clock was ticking as in a matter of hours Havana would be conquered by Castro and his forces. Batista wanted to bring along bags of clothes and other possessions, but Alverez stressed there was no time for any sort of delays:

"We must head to the airport now while the soldiers in the city are still loyal to your commands! If they fear that Havana is about to fall they could revolt or even worse join Castro and his men! We have no time to pack bags, you are a rich man buying new clothes and other worldly goods will not be a problem. Now gather your family sir; we must get to the airport quickly." Alverez stated.

"Alright colonel, Castro may have all of Cuba, but I will not be a victim of his bloody conquest." Batista vowed.

Marta appeared upset that she would be unable to bring several bags of her possessions, but Batista and Alverez both explained that it was more important to leave than to cling to material goods. Batista's two children were ready to follow their parents and had no idea about the great danger their family was in. Alverez summoned two palace guards to help escort the Batista family to the blue Cadillac waiting in front of the building. Radio reports were now starting to sound more urgent than they had just minutes before. Alverez would ride in the first Cadillac in the convoy as the three vehicles headed for the airport.

All three cars were equipped with bulletproof glass and armor plating. Batista was not a man who could afford to be caviler with his life. Alverez gave the signal for the convoy to head to the airport and ordered the drives to go as fast as possible. Batista sat back and silently reflected on his time in power. He had staged a coup in 1952 against the leader of Cuba and so it was somewhat ironic that Batista was fleeing from another military takeover of the government. Marta was more interested in the safety of the children and wealth that the family would require than her husband's power.

As the convoy headed through the streets the sounds of gunfire and artillery shelling increased. It was clear that Havana could not withstand Castro's dedicated forces much longer.

Alverez radioed ahead to the airport and informed the pilots that they should be ready to start the engines once the family was aboard. Even with all of the weapons that Castro's forces had none of them were designed to attack aircraft once they left the ground. Takeoff priority would be quickly given to the DC-7 once Batista and his family were aboard.

Radio reports were now indicating that Castro's forces had begun to enter the eastern part of Havana. Lucky for Batista the airport was in the western part of the capital. Alverez had served Batista for many years and believed that Cuba deserved a man better than Castro for a leader. For the moment there were more important issues for the colonel to attend to than his political desires. A security checkpoint had been setup near the airport. Alverez quickly lowered his rear window to speak with the guards. It took on a few seconds for the convoy to be waved through once Alverez explained who was in the middle Cadillac.

HAVANA AIRPORT,
8:24 AM:

THE SCENE AT THE AIRPORT WAS CHAOTIC AS PLANES WERE DEPARTING all over the place even on taxi ramps if they were long enough. Amazingly it had taken the Batista family only twenty minutes to get dressed and reach the airport as they had left most of their possessions behind. Alverez was first to enter the DC-7 and he made certain the pilots were ready to start the engines once the family was aboard the plane. Batista, Marta and the children entered the aircraft next as they quickly found their seats near the front of the plane. A few seconds later the air stairs were removed and the engines started as the front door of the plane was shut and locked.

Both of the pilots were nervous about taking off as they were concerned the plane might be targeted by Castro's forces. Alverez assured them that the enemy did not have antiaircraft capabilities. This assurance by the colonel was enough to ease the main concern of the pilots as they pushed the throttles forward. Clearance had been given to the DC-7 for immediate takeoff as it was one of the few commercial planes left at the airport.

Alverez leaned back in his seat pondering the fate that his beloved Cuba would now endure under Castro. The aircraft was headed for Miami where Alverez would be dropped off. Then Batista and his family were going to fly on to New York before heading out for their final destination in Lisbon, Portugal. A new life awaited all of the people aboard the plane including the pilots. There was no going back to Cuba for any of them.

Halfway down the runway the DC-7 finally reached takeoff speed which would allow the plane to leave the ground. The pilots gently pulled back on their yokes and the plane lifted off with ease. Batista and his family were now safe as Castro's forces could not harm the plane. With the arrival of the rebel forces imminent the men in the control tower quickly left their posts. They wanted to be nowhere near the airport when Castro arrived. It was well known that rebels who found men working for the government shot them on sight.

10 MINUTES LATER:

CASTRO ARRIVED AT THE AIRPORT IN A JEEP THAT WAS DRIVEN BY HIS brother Raul. Che Guevara was also in the vehicle and although Batista had escaped all of Cuba was now under Castro's control. He pulled out a handful of cigars and gave one to his comrades before lighting his own. It was a moment they had been working towards since the revolution began over five years earlier. Castro was the first to speak as he wanted to say something meaningful on their importance occasion that both his brother and Che would remember:

"Batista is a coward and has left Havana like a sacred puppy that runs away when it hears a loud noise. He did not have the courage to defend the capital to the death and that is why he was a bad leader of Cuba. A new era will soon dawn in this nation as we are going to be its founders and leaders." Castro commented.

"Cuba needs strong leadership and men of bravery which it lacked under Batista. He was a decadent leader that bowed before the United States at every turn. Cuba must be free of the corrupt influence of America. We are not a puppet nation of that land to the north." Raul added.

"The day of liberation has finally arrived for Cuba as its time under the heel of the United States is over with the departure of Batista. Comrades tonight we celebrate as our land is free of a tyrant!" Castro added.

"Our efforts in Cuba have been rewarded and the days of capitalism running this nation are over. The people will be liberated from the chains of private enterprise as it has turned them into sheep." Raul remarked.

Che was more reserved than normal and Castro did not press the matter as Guerra was a loyal patriot helping the cause of Cuba. Batista had fled Cuba leaving it to Castro and his victorious rebels. A new government would soon be formed and it would be centered on socialism for the people instead of capitalism that had been part of every government since 1898. Castro wanted to align Cuban with the Soviet Union as it was more willing to provide resources than the United States. Weapons and economic aid were the top priorities for Castro. He wanted Cuba to be strong and independent no matter what the cost.

Raul backed his brother and was ready to follow Fidel on whatever plan he had for the new government. This intense loyalty came from fighting side by side for over five years with his brother. There was a sense of elation by all the rebels as they had won and managed to force Batista to flee the country. Castro smiled as he looked at the nearly deserted airport. He enjoyed causing people to fear his presence and power. As the three men smoked their cigars they watched as fellow rebels celebrated the defeat of Batista.

MIAMI INTERNATIONAL AIRPORT,
1 HOUR LATER:

HAVING MANAGED TO SUCCESSFULLY ESCAPE CUBA IN ONE PIECE COL. Alverez bid farewell to Batista and his family before leaving the DC-7. His job as serving as the head of the personal guard was no longer required. Many of the Cubans who had fled from

Castro's advance were now in Miami. Alverez was looking forward to putting this tragic chapter of exile behind him. Running away from problems was never the colonel's style. He knew that Castro would impose his will on Cuba in a matter of months if not weeks. This new government would only benefit Castro and his men.

In addition to the DC-7 carrying Batista and his family there were several planes that arrived from Cuba with passengers fleeing Castro's advance towards Havana. Most of the people who managed to escape were rich, but some were middle income families. Alverez needed to clear his head as the morning had proved trying. He spotted the airport lounge and walked towards it hoping to forget about the last few hours. Batista and his family would soon be departing for New York. A new home was required for them and Lisbon, Portugal seemed ideal as it contained a similar climate to that of Cuba. More importantly Portugal approved of Batista's family coming to live there.

Alverez found the airport lounge to his liking as it had nothing to remind him of Cuba. Two beers quickly were downed by the colonel as he believed his actions should be rewarded. Batista and his family were still alive and well despite the efforts of Castro. As for his personal future, Alverez had not given the vital matter that much thought yet. In many ways the colonel was still in a survival mentality and this would last for nearly another day before rational thinking could take place once again.

Batista and his family ordered the pilots to takeoff as they were eager to get on with their trip. Alverez heard the engines starting up on the DC-7 and watched as the plane taxied out to the runway. For over a decade the colonel had assured Batista was protected from all of his enemies. A new chapter would soon be written in the life of the ever dedicated Col. Alverez. He was no longer the guardian of a leader, but his desire to assist Cuba would shape his next assignment in ways he did not yet know. Less than a minute later the DC-7 took off and began its journey to New York.

Many of the exiles from Cuba had also come to Miami as it

was the closest US city to the island. Alverez still saw himself as an officer in the Cuban Army. Others who fled the island nation were also thinking of their former lives in Cuba. The revolution that toppled the government disrupted the lives of millions as some had chosen exile while others stayed to weather the political storm that just took place. For all of them the days under Batista were over and an uncharted future lay ahead.

CASTRO, RAUL AND CHE ALL WALKED CALMLY INTO THE PRESIDENtial Palace before signaling for everything to be removed that belonged to Batista except for a golden telephone that Castro wanted to put on display. He intended to show the dangers of capitalism and how decadent the relationship with America had become by showing off the golden telephone. A rebel messenger arrived with news that the Soviet Union was pleased that Castro's revolution had proven successful. Seconds later a simple statement was given to the messenger by Castro that was to be sent at once:

"We will be in contact with you soon. With deep regards from Fidel Castro your comrade in the struggle against the United States." Castro stated.

"Yes sir, I will send this message right away to the Soviet Union." The messenger confirmed.

"Good, you are dismissed sergeant; I need time to redecorate this entire building. It must be transformed into something more fitting of a great leader. The stain of Batista must be cleansed from the structure. As for you two, pick out a bedroom and it shall be yours. The master bedroom is mine as I have earned it. With Batista gone his palace must be put to good use." Castro replied.

With Batista gone the people of Cuba held mixed reactions as some were glad the tyrant was gone while others believed a new dictator would quickly take his place in the months ahead. Castro was unknown by the people of Cuba except for the rebels. Havana was now secured and the other cities and towns throughout the nation were awaiting their new government. Castro, Raul and Che were to be the three leading figures in the new command structure of Cuba. They had all been at the heart of the revolution and each saw themselves as liberators instead of conquerors.

Castro was ready to embrace the leadership of Cuba now that the position had finally been obtained through force of arms. In an ironic twist when he was younger Castro had once been in a program to mold him into a priest of the Catholic Church. His early days of being a humble servant of the public were behind him. Enemies of the revolution needed to be dealt with and entire lists were already being drawn up. Raul and Che were eager to endorse Castro's desire to purge Cuba of its threats by bloodshed. The three of them each saw political stability as more important than civil liberties.

As for the lives of the Cubans in Havana they were not yet aware of any major changes. They mostly stayed off the streets and away from the rebels. All of them knew that the days ahead would see their reality change and none of them were sure in which direction it would go. Batista had enjoyed the excesses of life and everyone in Cuba knew of his decadence. Castro and his forces also had a reputation that was known to the people. While not overly barbaric the rebel forces were viewed as willing to enforce their ideology not matter what the costs. The word socialism had become more than a catchphrase for the rebels as to them it was a way of life.

LANGLEY, VA, CIA HEADQUARTERS, 4 HOURS LATER:

BATISTA'S FLIGHT FROM CUBA WAS NOW PART OF A REPORT ON THE stability of the island nation. An intelligence briefing would be given to President Eisenhower the next day and its contents would include the current situation in Cuba along with possible consequences. For the moment Castro was not mentioned as a serious problem for the United States. He was viewed by the CIA as just another revolutionary that would be taking power. Cuba had a US naval base at Guantanamo Bay which was created shortly after the 1898 Spanish American War. Batista was out of the picture and the fate of Cuba remained to be seen in the weeks and months ahead. Both Cuba and the United States were keeping a close eye on each other for any problems that might arise.

The report on the situation in Cuba had been written by Agent Jason Sims. He was a junior member on the ever active Caribbean Affairs Desk. This was Sims first major assignment and he felt highly driven to display his talent for creating a report. All of the details of Batista's defeat were placed in the report along with several possible outcomes of what might happen with Cuba. One of the scenarios predicted that Castro might become a dictator similar to Batista and ally himself with the United States. Another scenario saw the formation of a socialist type of government with Castro in charge.

All of the possible scenarios that were written by Sims predicted Cuba remaining on neutral if not friendly terms with the United Sates. The idea of a communist leaning Castro had not entered the mind of Sims or anyone else in the Caribbean Affairs Desk. Still it was too early for the CIA to get an accurate assessment of the situation. There were simply too many unanswered questions about both Cuba and Castro. Time would be needed before a better picture of the new government could be formed. Sims discussed the developing situation in Cuba with his boss Agent Peter Malone:

"Castro before today was merely another rebel leader that was fighting to overthrow a government. Now he has become a leader of a nation some 90 miles from our shores. Batista could claim many things, but being a great head of state was not one of them." Sims stated.

"That is true, but Castro might be no better than the man he is replacing. We know very little about him and until we do our assessment of Cuba is incomplete. The days and weeks ahead shall provide more details. Castro will be tagged as either a friend, neutral or enemy of the United States. That is how we classify all of the leaders of the world and it is our job." Malone confirmed.

Malone had been with the CIA since it was first founded back in 1947. His view on the governments of the world was based more on instincts that mere facts. Sims looked up to Malone and saw him as a mentor in addition to a boss. Cuba remained a nation undergoing profound changes to it. Castro was now in power and he would no doubt run things differently than Batista. Sims handed over the report to Malone who confirmed that it contained enough information to present to the president. Even some information was better than nothing at all which was part of working in the intelligence business.

Sims placed a folder with the name Castro into the file on Cuba and then moved on to another assignment. Malone had no doubt that within the coming weeks the folder on Castro and Cuba would grow in size as more details about the situation there were revealed. Sims was unsure with regards to what would happen in Cuba. He trusted the judgment of Malone and bet 20 dollars that Castro might pose problems for the United States. This bet was taken by Malone as he viewed the issue as not worth serious concern by the United States. Of all the nations to pose a problem for America it appeared that Cuba would not be at the top of the list.

JANUARY 7, 1959, HAVANA, CUBA, 10:00 AM:

CASTRO, RAUL AND CHE SAT AT THE HEAD OF A LARGE TABLE ALONG with several other men who had fought by their side during the revolution. Cuba required a new form of government to replace Batista's regime and Castro had decided upon a socialist dictatorship. Raul would act as vice president and Che would be a senior advisor. This left the presidency of Cuba to Castro. Other members of who took part in the revolution would also have roles in the government supporting Castro. As for the people of

Cuba they would now be guided towards away from the decadence of capitalism.

Castro's reign was now finishing its first week in power and he looked forward to shaping Cuba to his desires. Already enemies of the state were being rounded up for either execution or detention. Bloodshed was necessary to purge all elements of capitalism and loyalty to the old ways from the nation. Many of the victims were not truly guilty of high crimes. Castro simply wanted an excuse to remove anyone who might pose a threat. Raul and Che were glad to be on Castro's good side as to be his enemy could mean death.

Life in Havana was now drastically different than it had been under Batista. The streets were filled with men who served Castro and were looking for anyone who did not embrace socialism. Batista had been corrupt, but life under his reign was relatively peaceful. Castro was off to a violent start to impose his socialist government. All of the freedoms and goods that capitalism offered were now being replaced by monopolies run by the government. Terror was a way of life for anyone who did not submit to the state or attempted to break the laws.

To reinforce the message that Castro was sending to the people of Cuba radio and loudspeaker broadcasts were setup to praise the virtues of socialism. Freedom of thought was the first form of resistance to any type of government. Keeping the people focused on the benefits of socialism would help ensure they remained pacified. In addition to the propaganda campaign, Castro sent out men to gather information on the people. Informants were also rewarded to provide testimony against their fellow citizens. The old days of relative freedom were now nothing more than a memory. A harsh reality had descended upon Cuba in the form of Castro and his band of followers.

DOWNTOWN MIAMI, 7 HOURS LATER:

COL. ALVEREZ CAREFULLY FOLDED HIS UNIFORM UP AND PLACED IT IN the closet of his apartment. He could no longer serve in a military capacity as those days were behind him now. A job as a taxi cab driver now awaited the former colonel. This was a meager existence for Alverez, but at the moment there did not seem to be any other options. Personal happiness and survival were at the opposite ends of spectrum which Alverez had been through over the last week. For the time being making a living would have to come before his own desire to serve as an officer.

Despite his lowly status as a taxi cab driver Alverez kept a picture of Cuba to remind him of his home. One day the former colonel wanted to return to live amongst his people once again. Alverez headed downstairs as he had a job to perform. Driving around Miami was not the most difficult job in the world. Keeping boredom at bay proved to be the challenging part. Alverez had nothing against the United States, but it was not Cuba. Being among one's own people was something that could not take place in America.

The Cuban communities in the United States were friendly enough towards Alverez; however they had already accepted America as their new home. For the former colonel this assimilation into the United States was a sign they would never be going back to Cuba. With all the obstacles that Alverez currently had he still wanted to return to Cuba. This determination came from his former status as a military officer. A life of privilege could not be so easily forgotten. In addition Alverez also served the former leader of Cuba. This was not a minor post as it had offered great honor and distinction.

As Alverez reached the taxi cab he noticed some punks were leaning against the vehicle. This situation needed to be remedied as his shift would begin soon. All three of the punks looked like they were ready for a fight. Not wanting to make a big deal of the matter, Alverez asked the men to move out of the way. There was tension in the air as the punks looked towards Alverez:

"I have to get to work and you are in my way. Would you please step away from the car?" Alverez asked.

"We don't feel like moving right this second pops. Why don't you come over here and move us yourself? Do you have enough courage to take us on?" A punk asked.

"If you insist, I will remedy the problem that we seem to be having." Alverez replied.

Alverez quickly grabbed one of the punks and tossed him over the top of the cab. He then turned his attention to the other two and relocated both of them before they could offer any resistance. The struggle showed that all of Alverez's marital skills were still in perfect shape. Having dealt with the three punks the former colonel felt better about his day. While dealing with a trio of minor troublemakers was not particularly glorious it did remind Alverez of his former occupation.

JANUARY 30, 1959,
HAVANA, CUBA,
1:25 PM:

CASTRO MADE A CALL TO NIKITA KHRUSHCHEV AS HE WANTED CUBA to have support from the Soviet Union. Raul and Che supported the move as a powerful ally was exactly what Cuba needed. Khrushchev discussed sending over both military and financial assistance. Castro displayed his charm to make certain the deal went through:

"Comrade Cuba is a proud ally of the Soviet Union and will do everything in its power to enhance the cause of Communism in the Caribbean." Castro vowed.

"Your offer is most generous comrade. Our partnership is hopefully going to last many years. The weapons that I will be sending to Cuba in the months ahead are the best that the Soviet Union has to offer. As for the financial assistance it shall be around 10 million. This should give Cuba a chance to recover from its dark years under the reign of Batista." Khrushchev explained.

"I am grateful and delighted to be working with the Soviet Union. We are bound by both an ideology and a common goal to spread communism." Castro stated.

"That we are and our collaboration should prove fruitful to both of us." Khrushchev predicted.

"Good day comrade we will speak again soon. May our partnership thrive in the months to come." Castro added.

There was another reason that Khrushchev was helping Cuba in addition to it being a socialist nation. By aiding Castro the Soviet Union was gaining an ally close to the United States. This move would place the Soviet Union in a position to influence other nations in the Caribbean. Castro was a charming leader, but Khrushchev wanted more from his ally than to be flattered. Geopolitics was an important part of the Cold War for the United States and the Soviet Union.

Castro saw Cuba and its people as more than just another banana republic in the middle of the Caribbean. He viewed the nation as a powerful haven to spread to the influence of communism to all of South America. Revolution had forced Batista out of power and more revolutions could reshape all of South America. This goal was strongly pushed by Che Guevara as he wanted to liberate more nations. Cuba was only the beginning of a plan to spread revolution to over a dozen nations.

Castro was not as passionate about spreading more revolutions as Che, but was willing to support the idea for the time being. Raul wanted his brother to focus on Cuba and forget about spreading more revolutions. All three men had different agendas when it came to what they wanted for the foreign policy of Cuba. Despite each desiring something different Castro, Raul and Che all could work together towards common goals. They each wanted both Cuba and Latin America to be stronger than they current were. Nearly all of the blame was directed towards Batista and the United States.

CHAPTER 2

THE CUBAN PROBLEM

MARCH 15, 1959,
LANGLEY, VA,
CIA HEADQUARTERS:

AGENT MALONE AND AGENT SIMS HAD RECEIVED REPORTS OF SOVIET cargo ships heading to Cuba. This confirmed the rumor that Castro had become more open to communism than he once led on upon taking power. Instead of being merely another nation in the Caribbean, Cuba was now a base for Soviet operations and influence. Malone handed over the 20 dollars he bet Sims and proceeded to upgrade Cuba from minor annoyance to a national problem. In the CIA being classified as a problem nation made certain that the US Government would take notice and that all political relations were now officially cut.

Cuba in the last two and half months had gone from a socialist leaning nation to a communist nation. Castro had shown himself to be far worse than Batista as the political prisoners were executed by the thousands. Che wanted to begin spreading more revolutions across the nations of South America. Castro urged his comrade to stay in Cuba for a few more years. Rushing over to fight in more revolutions was tiring work. Castro and Raul could use all the help they could get in Cuba.

They saw Che as a passionate man who would ensure that any problems that came up in Cuba were dealt with.

The CIA saw Cuba as a problem for the United States and one that needed to be solved quickly. Castro was a leader that wanted to enhance the power of Cuba. If the Soviet influence became too strong than more nations in Latin America would fall to communism. Since 1945 the stated goal of the United States was to contain all nations that became communist. This strict containment seemed to be the only way of protecting the free world. If Cuba was not quickly dealt with it would serve as a match to light South America alight with revolutions.

Malone and Sims discussed possible options for how the United States could deal with Cuba. There were no clear answers as all of the options were only stopgap measures at best. Malone and Sims would be presenting their opinions to their superiors in one hour. A way of dealing with Cuba was needed and Malone outlined what he thought were the options:

"There are three options for the United States to pursue when it comes to Cuba. The first is diplomatic and it might provide a chance to talk Castro away from his link with the Soviet Union. The second option is sanctions from the United Nations to pressure Cuba into giving up its link with the Soviet Union. Finally there is the option of military action. This choice would be the riskiest, but also ensure that Castro and his communist government were removed once and for all." Malone remarked.

"Only the first two options are politically viable as the third option would damage the image of the nation as Cuba is not a true military threat to America in the same way that the Soviet Union is." Sims pointed out.

"Still the Cuban Problem is becoming more serious with each passing day. We are running out of time to handle the issue. Once Castro's regime becomes too large for the CIA to address then the president might have to turn to the military." Malone stressed.

Both Malone and Sims could sense the urgency to deal with Cuba was building up. With each passing week the matter became ever more difficult to resolve. A decision would have to be made on how to proceed. Senior CIA officials were going to inform Eisenhower of his options on Cuba. A red folder would be given to the president which indicated the matter was considered urgent by the CIA. Color coded folders had been used for decades in the US Government and red was only applied to the most urgent matters. The desire for meaningful action against Castro was prevalent in the CIA. Their agents always believed in decisive action whenever possible. This was the Cold War and bold moves were required.

MARCH 17, 1959, DOWNTOWN MIAMI, 5:00 PM:

A MAN IN A SUIT WITH DARK SUNGLASSES GOT INTO THE CAB BEING driven by Alverez. Instead of telling the cab driver where to take him the man handed the former colonel a card with the letters CIA on it. Not exactly sure of what this meant Alverez started the cab and began driving. The man in the back introduced himself:

"Mr. Alverez my name is Agent John Smith and I work for US Government. According to our intelligence you were a colonel in the Cuban Army working for Batista until a few months ago. You arrived in the United States on January 1st of this year and have been in Miami ever since that time. I know that a man of your military skills is probably not overly excited to be driving a cab. I have a proposal that you might find worth your time. Pull over and stop the car here. If you should decide to accept my offer then call the number on the card and say that John Smith is in the New World. I will then contact you again at a time of my choosing. You have a chance to leave this job of being a mere cab driver behind Mr. Alverez. I would highly suggest that you do not let this chance slip away for any reason. Cuba is suffering under the heel of both Castro and his men. I know that you care for both the nation and your own future. Give serious thought to my offer. History is made by brave men willing to step boldly towards danger. You can be one of those men and I can promise that our offer is far better than serving as a colonel in Batista's service." Smith explained.

Alverez was surprised by what had just happened, but also eager to learn more. A chance to escape his job as a lowly cab driver deserved his full attention. Alverez was going to listen to the entire proposal before making up his mind. Returning to Cuba and removing Castro were the only ambitions that the former colonel still had. He wanted to strike back at the men who forced him to flee to America. This strong need for revenge and to restore his pride drove finally pushed Alverez in deciding to call the CIA to hear out their offer. There was nothing for the former colonel to lose at this point. He could always turn down the CIA if their plan sounded too dangerous.

Spending the rest of his working career as a taxi cab driver was not appealing to Alverez in the least. He had served Batista's and such a position was hard to forget. Returning to a job that used Alverez's military talents was imperative for the former colonel. The agent calling himself John Smith had offered Alverez a way to move on with his life from its current doldrums. Such a chance would not come along again and Alverez was well aware of this point. He could move forward without anything holding him back as his very future was on the line. Going to work for the CIA sounded both exciting and dangerous which were fine with Alverez.

`3 HOURS LATER:`

WANTING TO END HIS STATUS AS A MERE TAXI CAB DRIVER ALVEREZ had called the number on the card Smith gave him. He was instructed to wait at his apartment until someone knocked on the door five times. Alverez heard footsteps outside and suspected that he was about to get a visitor from the US Government. For this important meeting he was wearing his military uniform as it gave him a sense of identity and confidence. Five knocks on the door confirmed that the CIA agent had arrived to speak with Alverez. He quickly opened the door and invited Smith inside.

Once the door was closed the conversation between the two men began without delay. Smith strongly suspected that Alverez would agree to the proposal as his job was to find the right people for clandestine operations. With a few carefully chosen sentences Smith got straight to his point with Alverez:

"Mr. Alverez, let me be candid. I have a feeling that you are a deeply patriotic man that wants to see his beloved nation of Cuba free once again. Castro is a tyrannical dictator and has only the interests of himself and his friends at heart. In addition I suspect that you want Cuba to have a more democratic government. The CIA is currently working on a plan to achieve those two goals. You have military experience that will be vital to this plan. In short the CIA is planning to launch an invasion of Cuba and spread a revolution that will consume the entire nation. We need someone to lead a brigade of Cubans. This force of 1,400 men will invade Cuba and spread a revolution that will hopefully overthrow Castro's regime. The CIA will provide all the weapons and training you shall need for this operation to take place. I was hoping that you would accept the role of brigade commander. Your rank of colonel would be reinstated as the leader of a brigade is a valued position. The chance to rid Cuba of Castro and his regime might not come again, so if all goes well the president will approve of the plan." Smith explained.

Smith waited for Alverez to think over the plan and the offer as he did not want to pressure him. This was a delicate stage of the conversation when Smith needed to let the plan speak for itself. Alverez could choose to turn down the offer or accept the offer and be returned to the rank of colonel working for the CIA. It did not take long for Alverez to make up his mind. For him the choice was between the life as a cab driver or the ability to wear the uniform of an officer once again. Such a stark contrast in future outcomes made the decision that much easier. Alverez made his choice in less than two minutes and gave an answer. Smith smiled as Alverez accepted the offer being given to him:

"I would be honored to assist this plan in any possible way as Cuba needs to be free once again. Castro is a man that is worse than Batista. Leading a brigade to invade my home is a task that I am suited for. What kind of air support are you going to provide for this operation once it begins to unfold?" Alverez asked bluntly.

"Several A-26 Invaders will be used for ground attack against the Cuban Army. They shall provide cover for the invasion force to move off the beaches. As the Cuban Air Force is small it does not have the means to shoot down our planes. Naval support will be a few destroyers that shall be attached to the invasion force. This should be enough firepower to ensure that the brigade has a chance to get off the invasion beaches. From there the entire operation will hinge on the soldiers of the brigade gathering support from the local population. Castro is not loved by all citizens of Cuba. Support for an attempt to overthrow him is bound to exist." Smith assured.

"This plan is risky, but nothing worthwhile in life is without risk. Let us hope that all goes according to plan when the invasion begins." Alverez added.

"The CIA is known for getting its way when it comes to foreign operations. We have an impressive track record that goes back to our founding in 1947. Cuba will be no different than any of our previous endeavors. We shall assist a small force and stir up revolution that will sweep across Cuba. The days of Castro in power are numbered from this point forward. All we need is for the operation to be approved of by President Eisenhower. He has the power to green light all CIA plans or stop events in their tracks. This entire plan and its outcome will soon be resting on his shoulders. I hope he approves as Castro is not a man the US can trust." Smith pointed out.

Smith was glad Alverez accepted the offer of leading the invasion force. A brigade of Cubans in the US would be trained to spearhead the revolution. This bold plan had been developed by the CIA mere weeks after Castro came to power. Smith was in charge of finding someone to lead the brigade and recruiting soldiers to join it. His main task now was to find Cubans willing to invade their nation and fight Castro. For decades Miami had been a natural place for thousands of Cubans to congregate in America.

Smith would be assisted in his task by several other agents of the CIA in his hunt for more Cubans for to join the brigade.

Alverez was going to be at the tip of the spear during the operation as he would lead the invasion. During his entire military career in Cuba the colonel had rarely been able to use his military talents. Now an entire brigade of soldiers was going to be following Alverez. This was a great honor and position of importance for the colonel. Smith knew that his instincts about Alverez were right all along. With the colonel on board the first steps had been taken to get the invasion from the planning stage into reality on the beaches of Cuba.

MARCH 19, 1959,
THE WHITE HOUSE,
9:30 AM:

PRESIDENT EISENHOWER SAT QUIETLY WITH TWO OF HIS ADVISORS LIStening to a pair of senior officials from the CIA. Operations Director Peter Jones took the lead in explaining the plan. The president had just finished his breakfast and was in a good mood. A red folder was on the table containing all the important information on Cuba and Castro since he came to power. Eisenhower finally asked the big question that had been on his mind since the CIA officials began their briefing:

"What are the chances of success if you carry out this plan in its entirety?" Eisenhower inquired.

"We estimate a 60% to 70% chance of success if the invasion force is landed unopposed. Surprise is vital to the plan working. If the invasion force is opposed by the Cuban Army than the chances of success drop to 20% at best due to the risks of an amphibious invasion. There is obviously a need for total surprise for any chance of success to occur." Jones stated.

"I will not approve a plan that has a 30% to 40% chance of failing. Modify the plan until the chance for failure is less than 20% and only then will I approve of such an operation taking place." Eisenhower stressed.

"Yes sir, we shall work on the plan until it meets your requirements." Jones confirmed.

"Good, then our meeting is concluded as until a better chance of success can be offered this idea of an invasion of Cuba must be tabled." Eisenhower concluded.

With a definite no being given to their bold plan both Jones and his colleague would have to modify elements to meet the requirement by Eisenhower of a better than 80% chance of success. Having served in World War II as the leader of the Allied forces in Europe, Eisenhower was well aware of the risks of a major military operation. He did not want a plan to be carried out that stood little chance of success. The history of the CIA ever since its creation in 1947 was filled with prominent successful operations. However even so there had been several CIA failures which Eisenhower could not ignore.

After the CIA officials left Eisenhower spoke with his two senior advisors to get their opinions on the plan that had just been proposed. Both Stevens and Burke were blunt in their views on the "Cuban Problem". Stevens spoke first and his words got right to the heart of the matter. He did not try and sugarcoat the issue:

"What has just been proposed is nothing less than a total overthrow of the Cuban Government. Castro will either resist this attempt violently or perish in its success. This is a departure from our normal efforts as in the past we have entertained only minor operations. What the CIA is planning here is nothing less than its boldest operation in its entire history. Unless all the details are accounted for the end of this plan might be total disaster. I believe you are right to proceed cautiously." Stevens explained.

Burke was a more reserved man than his Stevens and yet his advice to Eisenhower went along a similar line to his colleague. The CIA proposed a daring plan that had merit if it was properly developed. Burke drove home this point in his advice:

"I agree with my colleague, the CIA is not talking about a simple plan here, but instead a daring adventure that could backfire in major way. If you wish to proceed with this operation against Cuba, then the CIA must modify their plan or it stands a high chance of failure. Now if the plan is given enough attention by the CIA and all of the details attended to, there is a chance of a success that must be considered. Castro has become a problem than no one expected to be this serious. In the few months that Castro has been in power the ties between Russia and Cuba have only become stronger. While it needs to be modified the CIA plan might be our only choice when it comes to removing Castro. The entire government of Cuba must be removed and replaced to eliminate Castro. I would suggest that you give the CIA two weeks to make modifications to the plan. If they come back here and give you a similar pitch then the entire matter can be dropped as too impractical. On the other hand if the CIA is able to improve its chances of success then you should consider the option as viable." Burke added.

"Thank you gentlemen your insight is much appreciated at a time like this. If I could be left alone for the next hour, my next decision on the matter shall be considered with great care." Eisenhower remarked.

"Yes sir, of course." Stevens replied.

FORT OWEN, FL,
3 DAYS LATER:

FOLLOWING A SHORT DRIVE FROM MIAMI, AGENT SMITH HAD BROUGHT Col. Alverez out to a former base that was used by the US Army in World War II to train recruits before they deplored overseas. After the end of the conflict the base had been left to the ravages of time. As the land was right next to a swamp the base had not been torn down for real estate development. Smith went over all of the current events with Alverez as President Eisenhower had not yet approved of the plan. The CIA was working under a deadline of two weeks to modify their plan so that its chances of success would increase.

Under orders to only work on the general strokes of the plan until Eisenhower gave the green light, Smith was now forced to take things slowly. He would begin the recruitment and training of the men in the days to come. Alverez would work closely with

Smith and oversee the transformation of men into soldiers. Still despite this important step nothing further could be done until the president approved of the plan. Unless approval for the operation was given within the next month the entire effort would be shut down and filed into the dustbin of CIA projects.

Agent Smith was well aware of how an operational plan could end if it did not receive approval. He had worked on several projects that were ended in the planning stages during his time with the CIA. As for Alverez he hoped that Eisenhower would approve of the plan as returning to civilian life did not appeal to all military men. The colonel had served Batista and despite the job ending sooner than he hoped, Alverez was proud of his service and wished for it to continue. For enlisted men returning to civilian life was often a blessing, for officers it was a step down for most.

Alverez was too young to retire and that meant that if the job with the CIA ended he would be going back to working as a civilian. Being in uniform again made the colonel remember his pride and purpose which until recently had been in Cuba. It was fitting that the CIA were asking Alverez to lead an invasion of a nation he was forced to leave due to a change in government.

While Smith and Alverez were looking over the training grounds several other CIA agents were combing over Miami for recruits. Smith explained how the training regimen was going to take place for the men once they arrived at Fort Owen:

"Nearly all men can be transformed into soldiers if they are instilled with enough discipline over a period of several months. Soldiers can overcome nearly any obstacle that is placed before them. We will have two tasks here at Fort Owen. The first task is to transform the men into soldiers over a period of several months. The second task is to prepare those soldiers to take part in an invasion of Cuba." Smith pointed out.

"The first task can be complete with relative ease, how long will the second task require?" Alverez asked.

"For the Americans that stormed Normandy in 1944 it took over a year of training to prepare those troops for that invasion. We will have eight months if we are lucky and perhaps less if the CIA pressures the invasion to take place as soon as possible." Smith answered.

"Are those eight months enough time to ensure the soldiers are ready?" Alverez inquired.

"Those eight months are probably are we are going to get and therefore all of our training must be compressed into that time frame." Smith replied.

A time constraint was in place for the training of the men once they reached Fort Owen. Smith could not delay the operation as the decision was made by his superiors in the CIA. Alverez knew that transforming men into soldiers would be the easy part. Shooting a rifle was a simple task to teach compared to training for an invasion of a foreign beach. Smith and Alverez were soon going to be training an entire brigade of men who were hand selected to carry out the invasion of Cuba. Intense discipline and skill had to be instilled into each of the recruits to transform them into soldiers.

APRIL 2, 1959,
THE WHITE HOUSE,
11:15 AM:

EISENHOWER WAS ONCE AGAIN SITTING AROUND A TABLE WITH HIS senior advisors listen to the CIA officials. Two weeks had passed since their last meeting. In that time the plan was modified to ensure a greater chance of success. All of the changes were in the areas of air support and naval support to the invasion force. Eisenhower wanted to hear that the chances of success were now above 80% and if he did not hear that statement the entire plan would be scrapped entirely. Operations Director Jones laid out the modifications to the plan and what they meant for the chances of success:

"To ensure that the brigade has a better chance during the invasion we have modified the plan as you asked. More naval and air assets shall be used to increase the firepower thrown against the Cubans. The invasion force will be supported by a dozen A-26 attack aircraft and three destroyers. The Cuban Air

Force will be destroyed before the invasion begins. This will eliminate the threat of enemy aircraft during the operation. False radio traffic will be sent out a week before the invasion. This will be used to divert Cuban military resources towards a beach 100 miles from the Bay of Pigs. We believe these all of these modifications have changed the plan enough to ensure that it meets your request for an 80% chance of success. As there is a lot of work to do for this operation to be carried out we ask that you give us your answer on the project no later than a week from now. We will leave the modified plan here for your advisors to look over. Have a good day Mr. President." Jones explained.

"I will give you my answer inside a week. I must have time to consider the matter." Eisenhower promised.

"Of course Mr. President, this is an important matter that must be weighed carefully." Jones added.

"It shall be, good day Mr. Jones." Eisenhower remarked.

Jones and his colleague quietly left the room as they now had placed the fate of the operation in the hands of the president for a second time. The CIA planners had done all in their power to make the operation feasible. If President Eisenhower denied the project again for any reason it would mean the end of the bold plan to invade Cuba and overthrow Castro. As with the first meeting the advisors offered their candid opinions on the plan and its chances of success. Stevens once again went first as he always spoke directly to the point:

"It is clear to me that the CIA has placed a great deal of effort into modifying this plan. They have added several air and naval assets into the operation. Combined with the brigade sized invasion force and element of surprise the project stands a good chance of success. That is as blunt as I can be about what has just been proposed with regards to the modifications." Stevens commented.

"My colleague and I are of one mind when it comes to looking at the CIA plan. These modifications have made the project stand a better chance of working out in the favor of the United States." Burke agreed.

"I thank you gentlemen, your input is much needed at a time like this. I have not felt this under pressure since the Normandy Invasion in 1944. I must have a few days to go over the plan thoroughly. Giving an answer to the CIA at this moment would be premature. They have come up with a solution the Cuban Problem that might solve the entire issue of Castro. Still a rush to action is never in the best interests of the United States. This matter must be considered carefully. I will sleep on the issue for several days. The CIA shall get their answer before the ninth of this month. There are many factors to consider on this plan." Eisenhower admitted.

"We understand sir. Take as much time as you need to make your decisions. Lives are on the line as they were back in 1944." Stevens added.

"That they are and once again the choice must be made about whether to risk an invasion or wait. I feel the tides of history have returned to my shores. I can watch the waves in silence and comfort or send a force to counter them by force." Eisenhower stated.

"There is no man more qualified to make that decision than you sir." Burke remarked.

"I want to be left alone for the next few hours. I have a lot of thinking to do." Eisenhower said calmly.

"Yes sir, everybody out." Stevens commanded.

Eisenhower was in no rush to make a decision about the plan to invade Cuba. He would not be hurried along by the CIA no matter how much pressure they applied. The president needed to consider how much of a threat Castro was to the United States. A Communist nation only 90 miles from American shores was something to consider. Even so invading Cuba for having ties with the Soviet Union seemed an overreaction. The CIA was notorious for advocating the overthrow of any leader or government that refused to help the United States. This issue of what to do about Castro and Cuba was no different.

Elected in 1952, President Eisenhower was the second president of the Cold War. This conflict pitted America against the Soviet Union in a battle for control over the nations of the world. This war was not fought with guns and instead saw influence as the most important weapon. Cuba and its people were nothing more than a pawn in this game of worldwide chess. Yet Cuba's location made it noteworthy to this game. If Castro were to allow the Soviet Union to use Cuba as a staging ground it would place military assets only 90 miles from the shores of the United States.

Eisenhower saw Castro as a ruthless tyrant, but this seemed to be a weak argument for an invasion. Cuba had done nothing against the United States since Castro came to power in January. Still the CIA wanted Cuba to be a pawn of the United States and that meant that Castro had to be removed by force. Eisenhower knew the face of true evil as he fought against Nazi Germany and their leader Adolph Hitler in World War II. Castro for all of his terrible actions was no Hitler. Eisenhower would have to base his decision on the immediate needs of the United States.

Removing Castro by force was not some small matter as it meant Cuba would be invaded by a US trained force and its government replaced. Back in the 1920s the US had sent in the US Marines to replace many leaders all over Central America. Eisenhower wanted a good reason to remove Castro beyond politics. If evidence came to the president that the Soviet Union was planning to place military assets in Cuba then Eisenhower would act. He did not want the United States to be in the position of worrying about a threat only 90 miles from its shores if it could be avoided.

THE GREEN LIGHT

A RED FOLDER WAS CAREFULLY PLACED ON THE DESK IN FRONT OF President Eisenhower. This folder was marked urgent and its contents were all about Cuba. US Intelligence had recently discovered that several locations in Cuba were being readied for military installations. There could be no doubt that the Soviet Union was behind this as Castro was in frequent contact with their leaders. Eisenhower also read a report on the number of Russia cargo ships that were going to Cuba. They had increased to over ten a month. This recent intelligence report was enough for the president to classify Castro as a possible threat to the United States.

If the Soviet Union were to place nuclear weapons in Cuba it would present a grave threat to the United States. Such a move would give a first strike capability against America to the Russians. Cuba was no longer a pawn in the chess game between America and the Soviet Union. Castro and his regime were now a potential threat to the interests and safety of the United States. Eisenhower saw no other choice than to take action against Castro. He would not allow the situation to deteriorate any further. Action was needed and quickly. Eisenhower picked up the phone and gave the CIA the green light to their plan for the invasion of Cuba at the Bay of Pigs.

Having made his decision the president felt confident that the CIA could deliver on its promises. If Cuba could be restored to either a democracy or at least a republic than the bold plan would have paid off. Eisenhower was now committing the United States Government to direct action against Castro. Normally such a drastic step never would take place during peacetime. However in a sense this was wartime as the Soviet Union attempted to gain more allies all over the world. Cuba never longer was a neutral party. Castro had sided with the Soviet Union, a move which forced Eisenhower to take drastic action.

Stevens and Burke were called in to advise Eisenhower on how the situation would play out. As always Stevens was the first to offer his candid opinion on what would happen regarding the CIA plan:

"We can only hope that this plan unfolds as expected. The rest is in the hands of the CIA and their agents which no doubt are training a force to invade Cuba right this second. They are competent intelligence gatherers, but as military planners the CIA seem to lack common sense at times. This plan has all the basics nailed down that is of course if nothing goes wrong. As you know in military operations unexpected things happen and events spin out of control. The CIA is now enacting a bold plan to oust the Cuban Government. It might work; if it does then we can say that you supported them all along. If things go wrong however I would advise you to distance yourself from the operation." Stevens predicted.

"Mr. President, I would offer a different piece of advice. Instead of remaining on the sidelines, I think you should ask the CIA for progress reports on the operation every two months. This will make sure that no major problems have arisen that you are unaware of." Burke added.

Eisenhower would soon have to choose between the conflicting pieces of advice about the CIA operation. Stevens wanted a discreet distance to be kept between the president and the operation. While Burke advised the president to keep a close eye on the CIA's plan. Both of the advisors had merit in their suggestions. Letting an operation be run entirely by the CIA was a good idea if they could be trusted to carry it out properly. On the other hand progress reports on the operation might give some warning if things were not as advertised.

For the moment Eisenhower could delay the matter of keeping tabs on the CIA plan to invade Cuba. He did have other issues to attend to as president. Still within a week or two a decision would have to be made as to how much freedom the CIA was going to be allowed on the operation. Eisenhower felt that asking for a progress report was not demanding too much of the CIA. Even so the decision would not be made right away. There was still time for other matters concerning the president.

FORT OWEN, FL,
24 HOURS LATER:

AGENT SMITH AND COL. ALVEREZ WERE BOTH ECSTATIC THAT approval for the operation had finally been granted by President Eisenhower. Training for the men had begun with the first group of 200 Cubans now formed into a company at Fort Owen. In addition Major Rodriquez had been recruited to serve as a training officer. Like Alverez Rodriquez had served in the Cuban Army and was more than willing to aid in the overthrow of Castro. Several CIA agents were recruiting in Miami while a handful stayed at Fort Owen to assist in the training. Alverez was looking forward to seeing his countrymen once again.

Understanding the need to motivate the newly arrived men Smith addressed the Cubans. All of them stood in formation wearing civilian clothes. Each of the Cubans would be issued a uniform in the days ahead. Alverez and Rodriquez stood directly behind Smith. The speech was quick and to the point as CIA agents were not known for long winded dialogues. Smith did his best to both encourage and enlighten the Cubans:

"Gentlemen toward you take the first step towards freeing Cuba of Castro. The United States will train and arm each of you. In the end however the fight is yours to carry out. This goal is simple to remove Castro by force and to achieve that aim we have selected you. Ahead lies a future for Cuba without tyranny. Castro must go and this is the beginning of that effort." Smith explained.

There were cheers and applause for Smith as he let Alverez and Rodriquez takeover. Training the Cubans would take several months and in that time the CIA also had to outfit an army. Clothes, guns, radios and a whole host of other equipment were going to be needed. This was going to be the largest military force the CIA ever setup as in the past their efforts were smaller. Before the Cubans were taught military skills they would require basic conditioning. While none of the men were totally out of shape, they needed strong muscles and plenty of stamina for the training to come.

Alverez and Smith wanted the men to be in physical shape within six weeks. This was a realistic timeframe as in that period the average man could develop muscles if they were conditioned each day. New recruits would be arriving and this posed a problem. Until the entire brigade was at Fort Owen the military training could not proceed. Rodriquez solved this challenge by suggesting that each company be rotated through different phases of training. As the first company of 200 Cubans was ready it could begin physical conditioning at once. After six weeks there would be several more companies ready for physical conditioning. Alverez and Smith approved of the solution as it made sense.

APRIL 15, 1959,
HAVANA, CUBA,
10:15 AM:

CHE GUEVARA WAS UNEASY AS HIS INTELLIGENCE CONTACTS INFORMED him of American plots. Specifically the CIA had active plans to assassinate Castro. This intelligence was relayed to Castro who shrugged off the information as nothing he did not already know:

"Every day that I breathe there is a plot against my life. Such is the burden of being a great leader. There were 42 plots against Hitler during his life and they all failed. While I see myself as far more of a revolutionary the comparison is still worth making!" Castro laughed.

"The Americans are not ones to laugh at. They have ways of eliminating their problems." Che warned.

"You listen to me, I do not fear the CIA they are like rats that think they can take on the large cat. Instead I fear an insurgency in Cuba. This government is strong and well supported by the Soviet Union. Yet there must always be constant vigilance against internal threats. If you want to be helpful than focus your efforts on that problem. As for the CIA, I do not lose sleep over their actions. I have my bodyguards and my doubles. They should deter any attempt on my life. In addition I have spies all across Cuba that keep me informed. America might indeed want me dead, but the question is do they have the will to carry out the plan?" Castro asked.

"I do not know comrade." Che replied.

"Neither do I my friend; however in any case we must continue on with our lives. Now focus on internal threats as they can be more dangerous than a poisoned cigar or an assassin's bullet." Castro stressed.

When it came to his staying in power Castro did not fear a foreign assassin as much as internal problems. He believed that the greatest threat to his regime could be found among the streets of Havana. In many ways this was a reflection of Castro's own mind as he began his struggle against Batista back in 1953. Che on the other hand saw the CIA as a threat to be taken seriously and would not ignore their power. Castro could rely on his spies and saw the United States as incapable of harming Cuba while the Soviet Union supported it. This faith was not shared by Raul or Che who viewed America with great amounts of trepidation.

Castro saw himself as a great revolutionary leader who could not be stopped by any force. He wanted Cuba to be transformed in the 1960s as a socialist paradise. Che and Raul simply wanted the regime to survive even with the United States only 90 miles away. Still Castro paid some attention to Che's warnings. His personal security was among the best in the world and it had all been designed to throw off possible assassins. Protecting Cuba from any form of invasion was in the hands of the military. Assistance from the Soviet Union was vital to making the Cuban Army and Cuban Air Force more than mere token forces.

Che was eager to begin spreading revolution across all of South America, but he was asked to stay in Cuba by Castro for a few years. As there were no pressing plans which required his immediate attention Che agreed to remain in Cuba. His friendship with Castro went back years to their first meeting in 1952. Batista had just taken power in Cuba and Che saw Castro giving a speech. It was a moment that brought the two comrades together. From that time forward the constant struggle against Batista became all they talked about.

Castro, Raul and Che all saw Cuba as a nation that needed their leadership. Each of them saw a future in which a socialist paradise could be forged. Help from the Soviet Union would make the transformation possible. Castro was requesting both military and financial aid to be delivered to Cuba. As this was the Cold War the reply from the Soviet Union was always the same. If Cuba was loyal to Russia than aid would flow to the island nation without any further prodding. The payoff for Russia was immense as it was receiving an ally that could be used for its own purposes.

MAY 2, 1959,
FORT OWEN, FL,
9:00 AM:

BASIC TRAINING WAS COMING ALONG FOR THE MEN WITH TWO COMPA-nies of Cubans being physical conditioned. The CIA had by now supplied all the men with uniforms and soon weapons training would begin. The main firearms the CIA was going to supply to the men of the brigade were M1 Garands and M1 Carbines. They were easy weapons to train on and available in large numbers.

Heavy weapons such machineguns and bazookas would also be issued. More physical conditioning was required before the two companies would be trained with weapons. Smith believed that it was going to be another week before firearms training began for the men.

Spirits were high among the Cubans as they were looking forward to overthrowing Castro. Miami was full of men willing to join the brigade. CIA agents had no problems finding them. The actions of Castro were hard to ignore and this made the Cubans in America detest the tyrant in charge of their country. Training for the men at Fort Owen was still in its earliest stages and Smith knew that as the months passed by the difficulty would only increase. Alverez and Rodriquez were working well together as they shared a love of Cuba before Castro.

Most of the recruits were young and single as they were lucky to escape Cuba alive before Castro took over. For the men that were married they were allowed to go home to their families in Miami each evening. Everyone else in the growing brigade lived at Fort Owen. Each of the barracks had been built during World War II and yet they required only minor attention. Smith wanted more officers as in total 100 would be needed. At the moment there were four at Fort Owen. Promoting from within the ranks would become necessary to fill the shortage. Smith and Alverez discussed the training regimen to make sure that everything was going according to plan:

"We have the weapons ready for firearms training and in the weeks ahead the men should begin shooting them. I feel that the recruits are ready for the next phase of basic training." Alverez stated.

"I agree, the Cubans are coming along in their training and they will need to be familiar with the weapons. They will switch over to firearms training in one week. As for our urgent need for officers the need to promote from within the ranks is becoming more necessary by the day to assist our effort. There are five CIA trainers here at Fort Owen in addition to you and the major. We must have more officers to speed up the training as of right now we have too many recruits to keep track off. I have compiled a list 10 Cubans that will make very competent officers. You can add or subtract a few of the names, but I need this list to be implemented at once. We must have around 100 officers for this brigade to run smoothly by the time training is complete. For the moment we require 10 more officers. As the brigade slowly grows in size more officers shall be required." Smith remarked.

"I will see that the men are given the training required to turn them into officers." Alverez assured.

"Good, well I believe that all other matters can wait as we have tended to the most important ones. You are dismissed colonel." Smith added.

"Yes sir." Alverez confirmed as he offered a salute.

Alverez carefully looked over the list and saw that all of the names were good choices by Smith. The colonel saw no need to alter any of the names. Alverez went to the site where the companies of Cubans were training and discreetly went around collecting the men tapped to become officers. As Rodriquez and the CIA trainers were all busy the task of turning the selected recruits into officers fell to Alverez. He took the group of ten men to the edge of camp before addressing them. Unlike Smith Alverez felt it was important to give a longer speech that got the point across. The colonel spoke with a serious tone about the job of an officer:

"Each of you has been selected to become an officer in charge of a platoon of 40 men. If you pass the intense training and are approved each of you shall become a lieutenant in this brigade. Officers are leaders and must be better than the privates, corporals and sergeants they lead in combat. Bravery is not the issue as all men who wear the military uniform need to be courageous. Instead an officer must be a leader and a person who can both motivate and discipline the soldiers serving under them. If any of you feel that being an officer is too much of a challenge then speak up now. The training you all are about to endure is more intense than anything that has come before." Alverez explained.

There was silence as none of the men selected believed they were incapable of becoming an officer. Alverez suspected that not all of them would pass the trials, but for the time being they were all on the path to becoming lieutenants. Without enough officers the training of the men would be delay and that was something that Smith did not want to happen. Eisenhower wanted the brigade to be ready before the fall of 1960. Election time was not a proper moment to launch a military operation. Smith knew that the clock was ticking. Any serious delay was going to affect the readiness of the unit. Pressure would be on the CIA to have the brigade ready for action in one year or less.

MAY 10, 1959,
LANGLEY, VA,
CIA HEADQUARTERS:

RECENT PROGRESS REPORTS ON THE TRAINING OF THE CUBANS AT Fort Owen were encouraging. There were now three companies of 200 men in basic training. This amounted to a full battalion of 600 men in total. Another 800 men would be needed before the brigade could be deemed ready for final training. Agent Malone was impressed with the speed at which the recruitment had proceeded. Still there was plenty of work left to complete. By now the operation to invade Cuba had been given a code-name by the CIA. Operation Zapata was selected in reference to the famous revolutionary in Mexico during the 1910s.

Malone trusted Smith and Alverez to transform all of the Cubans into proficient soldiers. All of the agents assigned to the project were tasked with helping bring the operation to a successful outcome. In total there were over a dozen agents working on the project. Malone was keeping track of all the details to make sure that nothing went wrong before the operation began. As senior agent in charge Malone took his orders from the director of the CIA himself. All of the paperwork and money for the project stopped at Malone. He had clearance to make the operation viable.

Progress on training the invasion force was proceeding on schedule. Smith had stated to Malone that it would take no less than eight months to ready the brigade. This time table was acceptable as it fell in line with what both the CIA and President Eisenhower expected. All of the events taking place in Fort

Owen was being recorded by the CIA. They wanted to catalog everything that happened for future use if the operation was a success in overthrowing Castro. Malone was the first to know of any delays or setbacks as Smith kept in constant contact with him on a daily basis.

Wanting to put down his own thoughts on the project Malone wrote a few paragraphs on the subject which would be filed with his personal documents:

"Operation Zapata is an ambitious project to remove Castro from power in Cuba. The overthrow of an entire government is the riskiest type of operation that the CIA attempts in its line of work. Hopefully the fall of Castro shall follow the 1954 Guatemalan Coup. I have very high expectations for Operation Zapata. It is my opinion that Cuba presents a clear and present danger to the people of the United States. Castro should be removed from power and Operation Zapata was planned for just that scenario. Agent Smith is one of the most promising men in the CIA. His commitment to this project helps put some of my fears about success to bed. Alverez and Rodriquez are also competent officers. I could not have asked for a better group to lead this operation. Castro and Cuba must be separated by force of arms. If we can prevail the CIA shall add another operation to its list of successes." Malone reflected.

Malone was more optimistic than some of his fellow colleagues and placed the chances of success at around 80% for Operation Zapata. At the moment he had no reason to doubt that future events would unfold except as predicted by the CIA. Having worked for the CIA since its creation in 1947, Malone saw more triumphs than failures during his years with the agency. The culture of success was ingrained at the CIA by 1959. Dozens of small operations had worked out as planned which boosted the confidence of the agents and their superiors.

Operation Zapata was built upon the assumption that Castro could be removed from power by a small force of only 1,400 Cubans. This assumption was bold to say the least as there were millions of Cubans that might support Castro and his regime. The CIA expected that a small force could stir up support in Cuba and oust a man who was viewed as a threat to the United States. Intelligence on the citizens of Cuba revealed them to be willing to revolt against Castro. This intelligence was gathered by CIA agents and Cubans working for the CIA. There were signs that this intelligence might be faulty, but they all had been dismissed as unimportant.

HAVANA, CUBA,
2 DAYS LATER:

ONCE AGAIN CHE WAS CONCERNED AS HE SAW THAT THE PEOPLE OF Cuba were unprepared to defend themselves against foreign enemies. He explained his worries with Castro and attempted to convince him to arm the people of Cuba with guns. Raul and several other generals were concerned with this idea, but Castro wanted to hear more from Che before making up his mind. Che pitched his idea with a simple logic that was impossible to refute:

"America sits only 90 miles from our shore and their people are hostile to you and to Cuba. Since 1898 the United States has controlled the destiny of this island. Now your people are free and under your leadership. Do you want the United States to steal your people away from your grasp? Do you want Cuba to be stolen away from our grasp?" Che asked bluntly.

"No, it must never happen! Cuba must be free no matter what the cost! I must lead Cuba to a socialist paradise! What can I do to defend Cuba?" Castro inquired.

"You must arm the people of Cuba and organize them into local militias. The Cuban Army can only do so much to protect this island. The people must be asked to help defend Cuba. They are the strength of Cuba and with their help the nation can be defended from the terrible desires of the United States." Che replied.

"Yes of course. An armed people are the ultimate weapon against the United States. I shall do as you advise and arm the people. They will be formed into militias in the months ahead." Castro agreed.

Castro was willing to follow the advice of Che as it would ensure that Cuba could defend itself. Turning the citizens into members of armed militias was the best tactic to keep the United States from invading. Castro trusted in Che's judgment and believed that there was an imminent threat to Cuba. Ignoring danger at a time like this was not wise for Castro. Che suspected that all the citizens of Cuba would unite behind Castro if there was any attempted invasion. Propaganda would be needed, but the people could be motivated to do whatever was required in times of danger.

Che smiled as he was pleased to hear that Castro would be following his advice. Spreading revolution to South America would nothing in the long run if the Cuban Government was overthrown. Che wanted for Castro to remain in power for the rest of his life as it would ensure Cuba stayed close with the Soviet Union. Castro took out a cigar and offered one to Che as he wanted to celebrate the occasion. Accepting the offer Che took the cigar and struck a match to light his and Castro's. A few seconds later a conversation began about what prompted Che to be concerned about the need for armed militias:

"What prompted your recent suggestion about the armed militias in Cuba comrade?" Castro inquired.

"I have been paying close attention to internal security threats as you instructed and heard a radio transmission from the United States. They were attempting to appeal to Cuban citizens to listen to their lies. It made me think that the Americans might try more direct actions than mere radio contact with Cubans. If spies or commandoes were sent to Cuba from the United States you might be unaware of their presence until it was too late. By having the people of Cuba armed it would allow any strangers to be detected at once by the people. Turning the sheep into wolves is always a good strategy." Che explained.

"Good, that is excellent thinking on your part comrade. Cuba must be made strong from all of its enemies. I am glad to have you working at my side." Castro stated.

"I serve the revolution as you do." Che remarked.

"That I am certain of." Castro confirmed.

"May Cuba thrive under your leadership." Che added.

"To the revolution may it spread too all the lands that the United States has corrupted." Castro commented.

Castro and Che shared a vision of Cuba being a strong center of revolutionary ideas. The strong desire to keep the United States away from Cuba propelled both men to take drastic actions. Threats from external and internal methods concerned both Castro and Che. Arming the people was a step that not even the Soviet Union had taken during its existence. Cuba however was vulnerable to the United States being so close in proximity. Castro would trust the people to follow his leadership and not begin plotting against him. Che suspected that there were not going to be any internal threats to Cuba.

MAY 14, 1959,
THE WHITE HOUSE,
11:30 AM:

PRESIDENT EISENHOWER READ OVER A REPORT MADE BY THE CIA ON Operation Zapata. Agent Malone had written the report himself as requested by the president. Training for the operation was proceeding as planned. Intelligence on Cuba showed that Castro was continuing to import goods from the Soviet Union. This piece of information made Eisenhower reassured in his earlier decision to attempt an overthrow of Castro. In the Cold War the only two sides were with America or with Russia. There was no room for neutral nations. Even Switzerland and Sweden were nominally allied with NATO. The entire world was divided into two halves in the view of the Americans.

CIA agents were keeping a close eye on Cuba, but their main source of information came from informants. Eisenhower asked for a weekly briefing on the actions of Castro. He did not want to be surprised by any move on the part of the Cuban leader. Upon finishing the report Eisenhower jotted down his thoughts on the situation with Cuba:

"After over half a century of good relations with Cuba the United States is now forced into taking actions to overthrow the leader of that island nation. Fidel Castro is a man that reminds me in some ways of Adolph Hitler. While genocide is not an issue in this case there are many lives at stake in the current situation. As leader of the free world the burden rests on my shoulders. I have made the decision to attempt an overthrow of Castro. This action has been taken in the best interests of the United States. Before Castro came to power the idea of removing a leader of Cuba seemed strange, but now the concept has become quite easy to grasp. I only hope that all goes well with the CIA plan." Eisenhower wrote.

On most important events during his presidency Eisenhower had written down notes or personal thoughts on the topic. Cuba was no different in this regard as it had become another matter which required action by the president. The one difference was the lives on the line as both in Cuba and America people were looking upon the other as enemies or at least not as friends. Peace was still in effect, but the United States Government viewed Cuba as a possible threat. Eisenhower had taken the boldest step short of war to remedy the situation with Castro. Formers allies were both now on the path to violence and destruction due to their radical differences in types of government.

CHAPTER 4

THE MIAMI
BRIGADE

SMITH, ALVEREZ AND RODRIQUEZ ALL GAZED OUT AT THE BRIGADE OF 1,400 soldiers gathered before them and took pride at the sight. In eight months the force had grown from a single company of 200 recruits to its full combat strength of 1,400. This was a remarkable achievement given that only ten CIA field agents were assigned to the project including Smith. Malone and Eisenhower were also satisfied with the progress of the training. Still there was one task left before the brigade could be declared ready for the invasion. A regimen of assault training had to be completed in the weeks ahead.

There were now thirty seven officers for the brigade with 28 lieutenants, seven captains, one major and its commander Col. Alverez. Each of the Cuban officers had been thoroughly trained over a five month period. They could be trusted to lead their units into combat when the time came. Jungle camouflaged uniforms and weapons had issued to the all soldiers. Firearms practice was conducted twice a day. This made the members of the brigade proficient with their weapons as each man had trained 360 hours on them. Medics and radiomen were also fully ready to use their skills.

In addition to the assault training a name was required for the brigade and a conversation began on what to call the formation. Smith flipped through the CIA paperwork on the operation and finally spotted the official name for the brigade:

"According to the CIA the official name for this group is the 2506 Assault Brigade." Smith commented.

"That sounds like a typical government name; perhaps we can give it a little more of a personal touch. It should be named after the location where most of these troops came from. It should be called the Miami Brigade as that was the city where all the recruits were discovered. In fact the Miami Brigade sounds like the perfect name for this unit. Now if you will excuse me, I must oversee the weapons training of the first two companies. They all must practice two hours a day." Alverez insisted.

"Of course, carry on." Smith stated.

Smith was proud to see the brigade was now entering its final stage of training. Invading Cuba would place the daunting task of an amphibious assault on the soldiers of the Miami Brigade. To meet such a challenge they all needed to be fully prepared to overcome anything that got in their way. The US Navy would provide ships while CIA pilots flew the A-26 Invaders to eliminate the Cuban Air Force threat.

Training the men to hurry ashore and seize ground was the most important lesson they could learn during their time at Fort Owen. Alverez and the other officers had never taken part in an amphibious landing before as none of their combined prior experience came close to that area of combat. Even so the CIA instructors would have to educate the men of the Miami Brigade in how to seize an enemy beach quickly. Speed and surprise were vital to any invasion of Cuba. With only 1,400 men to employ the Miami Brigade could not afford to be bogged down a few hundred yards from the beach.

When it came to difficult military operations none were harder than landing on a beach under fire. The plan for Operation Zapata was to land the brigade undetected as this would enable the element of surprise to be used against the Cuban Army. If a large scale rebellion could be started by the brigade then the plan stood a chance of succeeding. The CIA had been very ambitious with their main goal as they wanted a brigade of 1,400 men to start a rebellion on an island of millions. Alverez and the men in the Miami Brigade were more focused on the training they were about to endure. Goals of the CIA plan were not at the top of their concerns.

JANUARY 25, 1960,
EGLEND AIR BASE, FL,
8:45 AM:

EIGHT A-26 INVADERS SAT ON THE RAMP READY FOR THEIR MORNING practice flight. These ground attack aircraft would be used against Cuba when Operation Zapata commenced. The A-26 Invader was a leftover from World War II as they served since the 1940s in the ground attack role. These planes were powered by two propellers and had a crew of three on normal flights. For Operation Zapata the A-26s would each carry a flight crew of two. There were to be the pilots and navigators. The pilots would also unleash the eight machineguns in the nose of the plane and fire rockets from the wings. All of the flight crews were comprised of CIA agents who had volunteered for the operation.

Practice flights three days a week were to take place in the months leading up to the operation. These flights were designed to ensure the flight crews had enough time to ready their skills for the mission. Taking out all of the Cuba Air Force planes was the primary objective of the A-26 Invaders. If possible ground support was to be flown over the invasion beaches. Once the planes were out of ammo or detected they were to proceed to their landing fields in Honduras. Agent Tomas Baker was in charge of training the CIA flight crews.

Baker was a man had seen his fair share of combat as he served in World War II as a B-24 pilot before signing up with the CIA in 1950. Now it would be up to Baker to make certain that the A-26 flight crews were ready for their mission over Cuba. He spoke to all the men before they entered their aircraft:

"Today is a practice flight gentlemen, you are to become familiar with low level flying and navigation. Keeping off Cuban radar is a must for Operation Zapata. During the actual operation this will be a predawn flight. None of you are to fly higher than 300 feet once your planes have reached open waters. If any of you lose an engine return to the base at once. Risk is part of the game, but so too is common sense. There are eight planes and that is enough to bomb the Cuban Air Force. Even with only six planes the mission can proceed. One more thing you all are to maintain radio silence unless there is an emergency aboard one of your planes. Now good luck and remember to keep low during all of your training. Success to you all gentlemen." Baker explained.

Baker watched as the flight crews boarded the planes and started their engines. He then headed for the control tower a hundred yards away. The A-26s took off in pairs as there was enough space on the wide runway to fit two of them side by side. Live ammo would not be carried until the operation began. The CIA had determined that the chance of an accident was too great to fly the planes for months with live bombs onboard. Fuel loads were also kept to only 70% of maximum to make certain that takeoff weight was not even close to fully loaded. Any accidents that happened during training might delay the operation and this was to be avoided if at all possible.

All of the A-26s pilots started their engines and went through the checklists to make certain the planes were ready for takeoff. Baker began to climb the stairs to the top of the control tower as the planes taxied towards the main runway. There was not a cloud in the sky which made it a perfect day for flying. Florida was known for its good weather during certain months of the year. Baker reached the top of the control tower and looked down at the A-26s as they reached the main runway. With their checklists complete the pilots could begin the takeoff without delay.

The roar of the A-26 radial engines reached a high pitch as

each of them were advanced to full power. Baker observed from the control tower as the first pair of aircraft took off. He knew that practice flights could be just as hazardous as the actual mission. In 1945 an entire flight of five TBM Avengers was lost during a routine training mission out of a Florida air base. Flight 19 had been a reminder to all pilots that even routine flights held the possibility of danger. Baker trusted the flight crews, but he also knew that when things went wrong with a plane at 300 feet a crash could follow.

CIA operations out of the air base were secret enough that the official flight plans for all the A-26s had been labeled as classified. The men in the control tower were aware that the flight would last several hours that was it beyond the general area the planes were heading. Baker had asked for top secret status as he did not want the public to become aware of the practice flights. It was a prudent move by the CIA agent. Secrecy had to be kept before Operation Zapata began. Castro was a dictator who kept informed of any action by the United States. He was not a man who let anything minor slip by his attention.

Each of the flight crews had been handpicked by Baker as he did not want the wrong kind of men to be carrying out the operation. All of the pilots and navigators were veterans of combat operations. Most of the flight crews had served in the Korean War. None of the men were over the age of 35 and none held a rank higher than that of major. Baker did not want to have colonels or old veterans be killed during the operation. The CIA was not in the habit of placing valuable assets in harm's way. All of the training for the flight crews was to be done at the air base as it was not open to the public.

FEBRUARY 10, 1960,
THE WHITE HOUSE,
12:17 PM:

RICHARD NIXON WAS RUNNING FOR PRESIDENT TO SUCCEED EISENhower and this caused an issue about the timing of the planned invasion of Cuba. Eisenhower wanted to discuss the matter with

Agent Malone who was now in the White House with a progress report on training of the brigade at Fort Owen. Operation Zapata seemed to be on schedule in the eyes of the CIA. Political forces were just as powerful as military ones in Washington. Having an invasion take place in an election year would be a risk by President Eisenhower to permit it.

A recent progress report on the training schedule of the Miami Brigade had just been handed to Eisenhower by Agent Malone himself. A candid conversation was about to take place regarding Operation Zapata. Malone sat down across from the president on a nearby couch and waited for Eisenhower to speak to him. The conversation began seconds later as Eisenhower got directly to his point of concern with Malone:

"According to the CIA's latest estimate the training of the brigade shall be finished by April of this year and they shall be deemed combat ready." Eisenhower stated.

"That is correct Mr. President." Malone remarked.

"What is the earliest that Operation Zapata could be launched after the brigade is finally deemed ready for combat in April?" Eisenhower asked.

"Depending on the weather the operation could be carried out within two to three weeks of the brigade being declared combat ready." Malone replied.

"Then the operation might take place in May or June if the weather forces a delay." Eisenhower commented.

"Yes sir that could occur forcing the operation to begin in June at the latest." Malone confirmed.

"That is in the middle of the election season and if a military operation were to begin then it would place the Republican Party in an uncomfortable position. If the operation was successful than there would be nothing to worry about. However if the operation were to fail then the political fallout would be directed towards both my administration and Richard Nixon's campaign. I am going to propose that the operation be delayed until after the election of the next president. This is to ensure that there is no political fallout which might seriously hurt the Republican Party." Eisenhower explained.

"Yes sir, we can delay the operation. However with that choice comes a higher risk of losing the vital element of surprise when the operation is launched. Are you sure this is what you want?" Malone inquired.

"I am certain. Now once the brigade is deemed combat ready keep it prepared for action. The matter must be passed on to the next president." Eisenhower answered.

"Very Mr. President I shall place the matter in the hands of the next person who becomes commander in chief of the United States." Malone acknowledged.

Malone was visibly disappointed that Operation Zapata was going to be pushed back until after the election in November. Despite this feeling he would carry out the order as Eisenhower was the final man in charge of all CIA projects and their timetables. Malone left the room knowing that the element of surprise might be lost if the invasion was launched at a later date. In addition there was the matter of seeing if the next president would approve of the invasion once again. Malone did not want to see Castro continue to tighten his grip on Cuba. The longer the invasion was delayed the more time that the Soviet Union had to forge a close alliance with Castro.

FORT OWEN, FL,
3 DAYS LATER:

AGENT SMITH INFORMED ALVEREZ AND RODRIQUEZ OF THE DECISION BY President Eisenhower to delay the operation until after the election in November. Doubts were raised about whether the invasion would take place at all by Alverez. Smith was honest with his answer as he looked at the colonel before giving his response:

"I do not know what this delay means." Smith stated.

"Clearly all of our effects here are at risk. There is no denying that this entire operation might be called off by the next president." Alverez predicted.

"I suspect that the invasion shall proceed under the next president no matter who that is. News clips regarding Cuba have been on the air lately. Both Democrats and Republicans are united in their distaste for Castro. It makes perfect sense as Florida has lots of voters who are from Cuba. Nixon or Kennedy for president in the end it does not really matter when it comes to Cuba. You can both rest assured this invasion shall be launched under the next administration." Smith insisted.

"I suppose so Mr. Smith; I would hate to think that all of this work and dedication has been for nothing. We have spent the better part of a year transforming these men into soldiers." Alverez commented.

Alverez was not as confident that the next leader of the United States would order the invasion of Cuba. He did trust Smith's logic however and placed his faith that no further complications would arise. Rodriquez was more pragmatic than Alverez as his career held more security than the colonel. Before signing on with the CIA the major had been working with the US Army in helping train their officers. Both men were eager for the invasion of Cuba to proceed. They each had personal reasons to dislike Castro and his regime.

Smith would address the Miami Brigade as he wanted to speak to them before the rumors gripped the entire unit with false speculation. Morale had to be kept up as it was one of the few things that bound all fighting men together despite their backgrounds or rank. Smith took a step towards the brigade and delivered a candid speech on what President Eisenhower had ordered:

"Men the invasion of Cuba is still going to occur as you have my solemn oath on that matter. The president has decided to delay the invasion until after the election in November of this year. This choice was a valid one as a military invasion must not take place in the waning days of a leader for political reasons. This brigade will get a chance at invading Cuba and overthrowing Castro once a new president is selected. For the time being we must all continue the training and prepare for that event. Focus on your training and the rest shall fall into place. Castro is the enemy and he must be dealt with." Smith announced.

There were cheers from the men of the brigade as they needed to hear that the invasion was still going forward as planned. Only the timing of the operation had changed as Smith was nearly certain that the next president was going to approve of Operation Zapata. Feelings in the United States against Castro were strong. Support for some form of action was to be found in both political parties to varying degrees. Smith would use the extra time to make certain the brigade was ready for combat when the moment arrived. While operation would be delayed the need for the soldiers of the Miami Brigade to remain prepared for the invasion persisted.

MARCH 15, 1960,
HAVANA, CUBA,
1:30 PM:

CASTRO AND CHE WERE ONCE AGAIN TALKING OVER THE NEED TO maintain the current internal security in Cuba. Armed militia units comprised of citizens were now to be found all over the island. Every major city in Cuba was ordered to form a militia and smaller towns also were instructed by Castro to create them. Che was highly confident these militias would guarantee the security of the government. Spies were important for gathering intelligence, but the best way to deter a foreign power was by force of arms. The citizens of Cuba were being transformed from sheep into wolves by Castro's regime.

Establishment of the militias was coming along rapidly as Che urged Castro not to delay on the matter. Other security measures were already in place to prevent any foreign power from toppling the government. Spies and informants could be found all over Cuba. Loyalty to Castro was absolute as he did not tolerate anyone who failed to share his passion for a socialist paradise. Che was beginning to enjoy his time in Cuba instead of seeing it as a detour away from his goal of spreading revolution across South America.

By now threats against Castro from the United States had fallen into a predictable pattern which the dictator began to accept as normal. The CIA was unable to get close to Castro as his personal security rank among the best in the world. Yet

Cuba still remained as a target for the United States as the Cold War raged on without any sign of relenting. Soviet transports were continuing to bring in military supplies and some commercial supplies which Castro requested. Che discussed the growing ties between Cuba and Russia. He was hoping to gain Soviet support for his planned revolutions:

"Cuba is being transformed thanks to your vision and the material provided by the Soviet Union. Instead of being a pawn for the United States, Cuba can be a nation that stands on its own two feet with pride." Che observed.

"That is true the support the Soviet Union is sending has helped improve Cuba from its previous state. Yet more is needed comrade as the socialist revolution must touch ever corner of this island. All of the people have to be brought into the paradise created by my regime. There can be no group of people that resists the spread of this government. Batista was a fool and ignored the will of the people. I on the other hand shall guide the will of the people myself. Citizens of any nation are fickle at heart and that is why a strong government must suppress any person that gets in its way. Small acts of defiance can lead to insurrections and civil war. I know of this as all of my actions against Batista were built upon small actions in the years before armed conflict. Now what did you want to ask me?" Castro inquired.

"I was hoping that the Soviet Union could support my revolutions in South America." Che remarked.

"For the moment my friend stay in Cuba, I still require your assistance in fighting my enemies. When the time comes I shall speak to Khrushchev about supplying you with some form of support for your desire to spread revolution across South America. Such ambition is a sign of a powerful man." Castro pointed out.

"Thank you, I feel my presence in Cuba is a learning experience for future projects." Che added.

Che was viewed by Castro as the perfect right hand man as he followed orders without question. Raul had to be enticed with positions of power to remain fully loyal to Castro. While Raul was Castro's brother they did not always see eye to eye on all issues. Che shared a similar outlook on the world as Castro and therefore they both held the same ideology. When it came to power trust was based entirely on loyalty as Castro could not run Cuba all by himself. He needed to trust all the men around him and could not elevate someone who did not share his vision for the nation. Che had plans that extended beyond Cuba, but for the moment he would stay and help Castro in whatever way the dictator requested.

APRIL 24, 1960,
FORT OWEN, FL,
11:00 AM:

SMITH HELD A STOPWATCH IN ONE HAND AND A CLIPBOARD IN THE other. The Miami Brigade was now in its final phase of amphibious assault training. Alverez and Rodriquez were pushing their men hard, but it was to ensure they could carry out an invasion of Cuba. Quickly moving the troops ashore was one of the most vital tasks. Groups of 40 men were lined up and ordered to dash through a trench lined with water for 150 feet. This exercise was to simulate what stepping off a landing ship would feel like when the time came. Wadding ashore had to be done in a rapid fashion. Any delay placed the men in the water at risk of being shot or discovered.

Alverez led the officers through the water filled trench first as he wanted to show that the enlisted men that he would lead them through all obstacles. Smith ordered the first group to go and started his stopwatch. A time of less than two minutes was expected for each of the groups to clear the trench. These groups of forty were the same as the landing boats were going to be filled with during the invasion of Cuba. Smith kept a very close eye on the stopwatch as he observed the exercise proceed. Alverez urged the officers forward and instructed them to lift their legs high to progress down the trench faster. Seconds ticked by and as the last officer left the time on Smith's stopwatch was one minute and forty seconds.

The first group had made it through the obstacle with

twenty seconds to spare. Now the rest of the groups were going to attempt to pass the two minute mark. Smith gave the signal for the next forty men to stand ready. Alverez stood next to the trench to encourage the groups and make certain they lifted their legs high enough. As Smith saw that the group was ready he gave the signal for the exercise to start. Once again the men set out to race to the end of the trench under two minutes. Alverez shouted at the men to move fast and keep their legs high to make better forward progress.

Rodriquez also motivated the men to make a speedy advance through the trench. It was important for the two senior officers to be seen by the men taking an active part in the training. Soldiers would go the extra mile for leaders that showed interest in them. Those leaders who ignored the care of their men under them always paid a price in discipline and efficiency. Alverez and Rodriquez were both hands on officers. The two officers always were seen by the troops and never asked anything of the men that they would not do themselves. Smith had selected both seniors based as much on their leadership qualities as their experience and rank.

Smith was impressed with the second group as they managed to complete the obstacle in one minute and thirty seconds. If the rest of the forty man groups could keep up this pace the toughest part of the training would be mastered by all of the members of the Brigade. Smith kept his rising expectations in check. He focused on each group that wading through the trench. Still there was good cause to be optimistic about this part of the training. The passion and discipline the men were showing was a very strong indication their morale remained at a high level. Smith wanted the invasion to take place as soon as the new president could authorize the operation.

45 MINUTES LATER:

ALVEREZ WENT OVER THE RESULTS OF THE EXERCISE WITH SMITH AS the last group had just completed the obstacle. Both of the men were impressed by all of the times as none of them were over two minutes. A few of the groups were slower than the rest, but most of the men had reached the end of the obstacle after one minute and forty seconds. All of the groups that were on the slower side would have to be improved. Alverez discussed ways to keep the morale of the brigade up during the months between the end of training and the invasion:

"We must keep the men here at Fort Owen for as long as possible once training is completed. If they are allowed to disperse in the months before the invasion the work that was accomplished here shall slow fade away. I suggest that once this unit is declared ready for combat additional training be scheduled to take place four days each week." Alverez suggested.

"That sounds like a good idea to me colonel. I will make it happen and get Agent Malone to continue funding this project in whatever way he can. The CIA does not want this operation to rust while the new president makes his decision." Smith acknowledged.

Getting the CIA to continue funding the operation was not a problem for Smith. He was on the good side of Agent Malone and had enough pull with his superior to make certain the money kept coming. The months between the election in November and a decision by the next president had to be ones of active training by the members of the brigade. Mental or physical rust of any kind would seriously harm any invasion attempt. This fact had not been lost on either Smith or Alverez. They both understood the need for constant training. As for the delay itself little could be done about its duration.

Morale among the troops in the Miami Brigade could be kept up if the new president decided to go through with the operation shortly after taking office. This was the one hope that Smith counted on. He did not want the new president to remain undecided on the operation to invade Cuba. Operation Zapata needed to be among the first items that was attended to by the new president. Amphibious training was nearing completion for the members of the Miami Brigade. This brought up the need for secrecy. If word leaked out that training was completed then the veil of secrecy about the CIA plan to invade Cuba might be shattered.

Smith had little choice other than to extend the training for the brigade. While the men would be able to see their families for three days a week soon the other four would require part time training until the invasion took place. This would prevent anyone from mentioning that the last phase of the training had ended. An illusion of training had to be kept up to prevent knowledge from getting out from Fort Owen. Trusting 1,400 men to stay silent on a matter this important could not be attempted. Smith saw deception as vital to the success of the operation.

All of the efforts of the men at Fort Owen could be undone by a few words that slipped out in conversation. This scenario had to be prevented at all costs. Smith informed both Alverez and Rodriquez of his plan to keep secrecy after the training completed its final phase. They did not want to mislead the men under their command, but saw the necessity to keep a tight veil of secrecy around the entire operation. Both officers agreed that the Miami Brigade had to be protected from its members talking when away from Fort Owen.

PRESIDENT
KENNEDY

AFTER EIGHT YEARS OF EISENHOWER, JOHN F. KENNEDY WAS NOW THE new president of the United States. Eisenhower had left a red folder on the main desk in the Oval Office. Kennedy saw that the contents of the folder were marked as urgent and top secret. He carefully looked through the pages and saw that a CIA plan for the invasion of Cuba had been prepared. Eisenhower had spoken of a project that he wanted Kennedy to decide upon shortly after becoming president. With his first hour in office not yet over Kennedy was approaching a decision point. Before he made any decisions two of his closest advisors would be consulted.

Robert Kennedy who was the president's brother and Robert McNamara the secretary of defense were among the smartest men in Washington. If a problem was given to them answers could be deduced in a matter of hours if not less time. President Kennedy would soon meet with his advisors to discuss Operation Zapata. Eisenhower urged Kennedy to act quickly and not discuss the issue with his entire cabinet. Secrecy would need to be kept if the operation was to proceed without being comprised. Kennedy like Eisenhower saw Castro as a threat to the United States if he continued to forge stronger ties with the Soviet Union.

Despite his dislike of Castro, Kennedy was not a man who trusted the CIA or military without question. During World War II a top secret operation to use an explosive filled B-24 failed killing its pilot Joe Kennedy. This was the president's brother and this tragic episode darkened the idea that all top secret military projects turned out for the benefit of their users. President Kennedy would not commit to any CIA or military operation that he did not personally believe in. Eisenhower approved of the CIA plan to invade Cuba out of national security concerns. Kennedy was going to require personal conviction in the morality of the plan before he authorized it.

2 HOURS LATER:

KENNEDY MET WITH ROBERT MCNAMARA AND DISCUSSED THE CIA plan to overthrow Castro. The discussion was brief, but to the point. Operation Zapata appeared to have all of its bases covered. Even so there were a few points that concerned McNamara. Kennedy was told of these concerns during the conversation which took place between the two men. McNamara viewed the world through numbers and logic as much as Kennedy viewed it through passion and conviction. McNamara was blunt in his assessment of the plan:

"This Operation Zapata is the boldest CIA project I have ever heard of. It has a high risk high reward style to it that smacks of playing loose and fast with the typical rules the CIA operates by. Having said that you must weigh that opinion with the fact that this operation also has a chance at getting rid of Castro and removing Cuba from its close ties with the Soviet Union. While the CIA report tells you that the chances of success are good, I know better from my own experience. There is another side that is not being told to you." McNamara remarked.

"Are you saying the CIA report on Operation Zapata is holding back vital information?" Kennedy asked.

"All governments always overestimate their abilities. I saw the same thing in World War II. We claimed daily that our B-29s could dunk a donut into a cup of coffee from 20,000 feet up. The reality was that average bombs dropped from planes fell 1,200 from the target. Bombs that missed by over 2,400 were counted in 50% their actual rate and bombs that missed by over 5,000 feet were counted at 5% their actual rate. That was just over Germany where missing the target actually mattered. I was stationed at statistics for our bombing over Japan where even a bomb that missed started a fire or killed civilians who were working for the government or the arms production. While the CIA plan might be accurate it also is leaving out numbers they do not want you to hear about. They have cherry picked the data and put together their best presentation." McNamara explained.

"I thank you for your candid assessment. Castro is a man who is terrorizing the people of Cuba. More importantly the Soviet Union is making stronger ties with Cuba each day that passes. If this cycle is not stopped we may be looking at nuclear weapons parked in Cuba and that is a threat we want to avoid at all costs. The CIA might have cooked up a plan, but the decision to employ this plan falls on my shoulders. I believe that Castro is more than a mere dictator. He is a man who could endanger the US and invite a situation which may start World War III. My decision is guided by those facts. I am going to approve of Operation Zapata despite the risks. If it works than the CIA can continue to boast of its wonderful planning. If this plan fails lives will be lost and Castro shall still be in power in Cuba. However to sit here and do nothing would be the greatest failure of all." Kennedy reasoned.

"I understand Mr. President. Castro must be dealt with no matter what the risks as he is a direct threat to the United States. The CIA has created a well-crafted plan, but as you well know it is not perfect. By the numbers it has a fair chance of succeeding." McNamara added.

"Yes, that is why I am approving of Operation Zapata as of tomorrow morning." Kennedy confirmed.

Kennedy had decided that Operation Zapata was worth the

risks and would approve it the next day. He wanted to show that the United States could deal with Castro by force instead of allowing the dictator to remain in power in the strategically important Cuba. This was the first major decision that Kennedy would be making during his time as president. Democrats were eager to show that they were just as aggressive against the Soviet Union and its allies as the Republicans. Getting rid of Castro would give Kennedy political clout and deal with a growing problem before it became too large.

JANUARY 25, 1961,
FORT OWEN, FL,
8:30 AM:

SMITH STOOD IN FRONT OF THE BRIGADE WHICH HAD BEEN TRAINING for over a year and smiled as he was about to inform them of very good news. He did not attempt to beat around the bush and got straight to his point as it was worth sharing for all to hear:

"President Kennedy has approved of Operation Zapata which means very soon all of your efforts here and all of your sacrifices during this past year shall be rewarded in full when the invasion takes place. All of you have been waiting for this good news. Removing Castro and having Cuba return to a more democratic government is what each of you desire as does the United States. This unit is combat ready and President Kennedy has been told of this fact. On his orders we shall put this operation into action and launch an invasion of Cuba. I could not have asked for you to give anything further to this project. You have dedicated your time and energy as that is all that is needed." Smith announced.

With Kennedy having approved of Operation Zapata the morale among the Miami Brigade soared to a new high as the invasion was finally going to happen. All that remained was for a firm date to be set for the operation to begin. Smith spoke with Alverez as he wanted to be sure that the brigade was ready in every possible way for the invasion:

"I have waited for this moment for two long years now and

it is good to see that the operation is finally moving forward towards its start date. As for the brigade I need to know if the men are prepared. I have reported that this unit is ready for combat. I have done all in my power to ensure the men have been trained and equipped for their mission in Cuba. However if any major or minor detail has been overlooked the entire operation could fail. You have spent more time among the members of the unit than I could begin to. Are they ready to carry out this operation in every aspect of combat?" Smith inquired.

"Yes Mr. Smith in answer to your question the men of Miami Brigade are fully ready for combat. They have been trained and equipped and only require the date of the invasion to be set." Alverez replied.

"That is all I wanted to hear. You may continue with your normal routine, I have to contact Washington and give them an update." Smith stated.

"For the record this is a moment I have been looking forward to as well. Cuba deserves to be liberated from Castro and his tyrannical government." Alverez added.

The men of Miami Brigade were ready to invade their native land and the US Government prepared to get the entire operation swinging into action. By now the project had grown into an impressive undertaking which no less than 25 million dollars was invested into it. Kennedy and his cabinet were eager to get the operation underway as they believed Castro was becoming a true menace to the national security of the United States. Smith would urge his superiors to request a target date for the invasion. Keeping up the training regimen was becoming nothing more than a stalling tactic.

Time had become a major factor in Operation Zapata just as much as the men and political considerations. The element of surprise was vital if the invasion was to stand any chance of success. More importantly the operation needed to be launched before momentum in Washington began to slow to a crawl. Smith and Alverez were aware of the ticking clock. Kennedy was less than a week into his time as president. Still there was a sense of urgency that could be felt by all in the White House.

More than anyone the CIA also wanted the operation to begin. They had as much riding on the project as the men who would be placing their lives at stake.

If Castro could be removed from power then it would demonstrate that the United States had total control over events in the western hemisphere. At the moment Cuba remained a constant reminder that the power of both the United States and CIA could be thwarted. Kennedy wanted to remedy this problem. Eisenhower had gotten the ball rolling and now it was up to the new leader of the United States to finish the job. Alverez saw Kennedy as a president who represented the United States in its purest form. The quest for democracy and freedom were ones all the members of the Miami Brigade sought. They would bring those ideals to Cuba during the invasion.

Reshaping Cuba was a strong motivation for all the men of the Miami Brigade. Nearly all of the men in the unit had lived under Batista or escaped from Castro's regime. They were fully aware of the life that every man, woman and child awoke to in Cuba. Making those lives better had become a mild obsession for the men of the brigade. Living in America had brought clarity to those that escaped Castro. Since fighting off the Spanish back in 1898 the Cuban people had been linked to America. Now that link was broken due the actions of Castro and his regime. The men of the Miami Brigade wanted to restore Cuba to its existence before Castro. It was this goal which drove each of them to place their very lives on the line.

FEBRUARY 12, 1961,
HAVANA, CUBA,
2:35 PM:

CASTRO WAS KEEPING A CLOSE EYE ON EVERY MOVE THAT KENNEDY made. He had dismissed Eisenhower as an old man that was not very dangerous. Kennedy on the other hand was young and appeared to be serious about his intent to bring America into a new frontier. Castro worried that his government was going to be a target of Kennedy's ambitions. This assessment was correct as a nation aligned with the Soviet Union could never be ignored by the United States. A conversation was started with Che about what Kennedy might do during his first several months in office:

"There is no doubt in my mind that Kennedy is going to be more aggressive than his predecessor. Eisenhower for all of the military experience proved to be a tame leader for the United States. Kennedy appears to be a man with plenty of passion in his belly. It seems to me that he has something to prove. What are your thoughts on the new leader of America?" Castro asked.

"You are right to view Kennedy as a passionate man as that is exactly what he is. He wants to lead America into a new era. I watched his speech when he was sworn in as president and got the impression that our dealings with the United States are going to take a sharp turn for the worse in months ahead. Kennedy is a man that wants to confront problems instead of avoiding them. Cuba is going to be at the top of his agenda as we have ties with the Soviet Union. You are also going to be a top priority for the United States to get rid of. I would strongly advise that you stay on guard for these next few months. Until our spies and informants get a better idea of what Kennedy might attempt nothing can be ruled out as impossible from this leader." Che answered.

"Yes of course, I believe that Kennedy is a man who must be watched closely. The United States is not the type of nation who ignores problems. Cuba must be protected from all threats." Castro stressed.

"Just be careful for the next few months, I foresee more trouble from America than we have seen in the past year. Kennedy might attempt drastic action." Che warned.

Castro took Che's warning seriously as Kennedy had proven himself to be a brave leader in World War II. This distinguished war record convinced Castro that more aggressive actions could be expected by America in the near future. By now the Cuban people were part of militias that covered every major and minor city. Che was impressed with the speed all the militias had been formed and equipped. Castro had placed his brother Raul in charge of the militias as he needed someone he could trust in command of the force.

Che predicted that if President Kennedy did not take any aggressive against Cuba in the next few months that none would be taken during his presidency. This hunch was based on how Che perceived the American leader. Kennedy was a very different man from Eisenhower and had something to prove as a leader. For Castro and Che the need for accurate intelligence now grew even more important than before. The United States was not a foe that could be easily stopped if it unleashed its military upon Cuba. Help from the Soviet Union was not enough as the people of the island nation were the first line of defense against any invasion.

Castro took a cigar and placed it in his mouth before walking to the window to look out towards the ocean. He quickly lit the cigar and wondered if the Cuban people could hold out against the United States. It was a matter that concerned the dictator greatly. All the militias in Cuba were no match for the US Marines or US Army. Without some element of luck to tip the balance it seemed that Castro was playing with a losing hand. Yet he was confident that his nation would fight like fanatics to oppose the United States in a direct conflict.

FEBRUARY 19, 1961,
THE WHITE HOUSE,
8:35 AM:

KENNEDY HAD SELECTED A DATE FOR OPERATION ZAPATA TO BEGIN after receiving subtle pressure from the CIA. The invasion of Cuba would commence on April 17. With a launch date set the only thing left for Kennedy to do was wait for the operation to unfold. Eliminating Castro had become a primary goal of the Kennedy Administration as he desired that the problems with Cuba be dealt with quickly. Operation Zapata seemed to offer all the good solutions with little risk. Kennedy was confident the CIA could pull off what they were promising. As this project was the first that the president authorized he desired it to turn out as planned.

Several intelligence reports on Cuba and a folder with an update on the Miami Brigade lay on the main desk in the Oval Office. Kennedy was a thorough reader and went over all the information that came across his desk.

The most recent projection by the CIA was that a large number of Cubans would join the invaders and start a revolution against Castro. This information had been compiled in Langley, VA which caused Kennedy to believe it was more of a guess than a fact. However the president badly wanted the operation to succeed and thus trusted in the CIA report.

While President Kennedy viewed the intelligence as being less than accurate he had no other information to form an opinion by. The Pentagon had given control of the operation to the CIA. This left Kennedy relying on information that was suspect to provide him with an understanding of what was happening. He wrote down his thoughts on Operation Zapata as this was his first major decision since taking office as president:

"I have finally set a date for Operation Zapata to begin. While the CIA assures me of their plan my two senior advisors have their own opinions. The attorney general believes the entire operation is foolish and should be abandoned. His reasoning is that the United States does not have the moral high ground. The secretary of defense sees the operation as being doable, but does not place much stock in what the CIA claims. Both of these men I trust and yet my own feelings have become part of this operation as well. I want Castro gone and as this project was handed to me by Eisenhower it seemed worth going forward with it. Cuba is a nation that lies only 90 miles from the shores of the United States. It has aligned itself with the Soviet Union. Castro is not a man that can be trusted to be a quiet neighbor. These are the facts of the current situation and they are undisputed. I only had two choices when it came to Operation Zapata. Either I went forward with the plan or scrapped the entire effort. While I suspect the CIA has not provided the whole truth on the matter, they are the experts in this type of affair. I have a feeling that not everything is going to go according to plan, but that is a risk that must be taken. Doing nothing is an option that I refuse to take when it comes to Castro. While Neville Chamberlin has since been painted as the man who appeased Hitler at the time he was cheered as having secured peace. I want peace with Cuba and that means that Castro needs to go as he is gaining more and more support from the Soviet Union." Kennedy wrote.

Kennedy's written thoughts on Operation Zapata were a candid opinion and kept with his personal reflections. He felt the CIA had not been fully honest about their calculations; however it was too late to begin asking questions at this point. All of the men at the CIA were old hands when it came to operations that dealt with affecting other governments. Kennedy felt somewhat out of the loop as he had just been asked to give the order to proceed. Even so the president's basic understanding of Operation Zapata allowed him to get a sense of all the working parts of the project. There was no denying that the bold plan to remove Castro had been given a lot of thought and consideration.

FEBRUARY 25, 1961,
EGLEND AIR BASE, FL,
5:00 AM:

EIGHT A-26S TOOK TO THE SKIES AND BEGAN HEADING FOR THEIR practice targets located in a small group of islands only 50 miles from Cuba. Low level flying had become routine for the pilots of the attack planes. They were now all flying at an altitude of 200 feet on a weekly basis. When Operation Zapata took place the pilots had two objectives. First was the destruction of the Cuban Air Force while it was still on the ground and vulnerable to strafing attacks. Second was to provide the landing ships with air cover. If there were any enemy planes sighted the A-26s were to leave Cuban airspace at once and head for their landing fields in Honduras.

None of the A-26s were equipped with tail guns or any other

defensive armaments which made them slow and vulnerable if attacked by Cuban jets. If the Cuban planes could be destroyed on the ground the A-26s could use their remaining ordinance on any Cuban ground targets that were in the Bay of Pigs. All of the pilots were under strict orders by Kennedy to leave Cuban airspace at once if engaged by enemy planes. While these seemed more like common sense than a necessary order the CIA pilots were all combat veterans. They were used to staying over a target area until all ammo had been expended. Kennedy was aware of this fact and that is why he had given the order himself as he did not want any sense of duty getting in the way of survival.

President Kennedy ordered that only one strafing run attempt to destroy the Cuban Air Force be made. He did not want to place the pilots in further danger by asking them to fly back over their targets for a second time. This did however place the pilots in the position of having to destroy all the Cuban planes on the ground in only one strafing pass. While each of the planes carried plenty of firepower they would be exposed to ground fire if forced to fly a second strafing run. Once the element of surprise was gone the A-26s were easy targets to any Cuban gunner that could pull the trigger.

Agent Baker was aboard the lead plane as he wanted to watch the strafing run on the targets. This was the first time that Baker had set foot in an A-26 since 1945 when his last mission over Germany was completed. Crammed in the cockpit behind the pilot Baker stayed silent as he did not want to disturb the flight crew. He was there to observe their performance and offer an assessment once the flight had ended. On this flight wooden targets in the shape of planes were setup for the A-26s to strafe. Baker was curious to see just how good the pilots were after several months of practicing.

15 MINUTES LATER:

AS THE EIGHT A-26S NEARED THE TARGETS RADIO SILENCE WAS quickly broken by the pilots. They each confirmed that their planes were ready for the strafing run. Baker took out a clipboard and pencil. He would score the pilots on their accuracy and time spent over the target. Although this was a practice run the pilots were all treating the situation as if it were the actual operation. Rockets were fired by the pilots first as they had a range of 2.5 miles and could reach the targets in mere seconds. Once all of the rockets were fired the pilots would open up on the practice targets with their nose mounted machineguns. Now the A-26s descended from 200 feet to 100 feet to line up their guns.

Baker looked over the pilot's shoulder to get a better view of the practice strafing run. The planes descended to 50 feet to improve their accuracy. Coming over the target it became clear why the A-26 was an effective aircraft for strafing ground targets. All of the wooden planes had been blown to pieces and Baker confirmed that each of the targets were hit multiple times. It was a perfect strafing run by the pilots. Now all they had to do was repeat this performance during the actual operation. Baker checked off all the boxes on his clipboard and told the pilot to lead the squadron back to the air base.

Baker was pleased with the pilots as they managed to exceed his expectations. All of the scores were higher than average putting the squadron among the best that was ever trained by Baker. The A-26s were still proving their worth over two decades after being used to fight in World War II. As the planes headed back to the air base Baker decided to announce his findings while they were still in the air instead of waiting until after the flight:

"Gentlemen each of you have proven that these practice runs have paid off. The scores I have marked down on my clipboard confirm that this squadron is ready for Operation Zapata. You should prove invaluable to the men of Miami Brigade. All of you have performed well and I expect nothing less when the operation takes place for real in a few months. President Kennedy has ordered you to fly only one strafing pass on the airfields. This is all you are going to require as I have seen for myself how effective these planes can be even after twenty years of service. Good work and keep it up." Baker explained.

There were a set of cheers let out by the pilots of the other planes along with the navigators. They were all feeling under pressure to perform well and this was now confirmed by Baker. When Operation Zapata took place the A-26s would be the first to strike at Cuba and each of them were vital to help pave the way for the landings at the Bay of Pigs. Disabling the Cuban Air Force had to be complete before the landing ships entered range of the beaches or they would be easy targets. This was the main objective of the A-26s and their flight crews were well aware of how important their assignment was.

FEBRUARY 28, 1961,
FORT OWEN, FL,
8:30 AM:

HAVING COMPLETED ALL OF ITS TRAINING REQUIRED FOR THE OPERA-tion all the members of Miami Brigade would soon be airlifted to Guatemala. Smith and Alverez discussed the imminent move to the staging ground:

"We have come a long way since two years ago when this force did not even exist." Smith remarked.

"That we have, I have gone from a colonel to a taxi cab driver to a colonel once again. Leading men in combat is a role I was born for. Castro is a man that deserves to be removed from power. For all the crimes that Batista had committed during his years in power Castro has already topped that number several times over." Alverez stated.

"I am glad that President Kennedy was willing to listen to the CIA and Eisenhower regarding this operation. To scrap the entire project would have been a cruel blow to the men of Miami Brigade. They have worked hard for the invasion of their home. While Kennedy does not want any Americans taking part in the invasion itself, I feel that Miami Brigade has been my greatest project since joining the CIA." Smith added.

"You and the agency have done well as we have enough weapons and supplies to carry out the invasion. I thank you for all your assistance during these past two years. Cuba is not the most important nation in the world, but to me and the men of the Miami Brigade it is home. We want to liberate our people and get rid of Castro once and for all." Alverez stressed.

"The men will get their chance to spread freedom. You will all get your chance to spread freedom as the results of Operation Zapata are going to provide a new chapter in the history books. Another dictator shall be removed from power by a brigade of 1,400 men who stirred up a revolution against him. The days of Castro in power are numbered." Smith assured.

Both Smith and Alverez were eagerly looking forward to Operation Zapata. They had invested all of themselves into the project and desired to see positive results. These also went for the members of the Miami Brigade as it was their efforts upon which the CIA was counting for its plan to succeed. Once the brigade had been moved to the staging area in Guatemala it would prepare for the invasion of Cuba in mid-April. The CIA had selected a staging ground in Guatemala as it had a harbor to bring the landing ships close to shore. In addition the buildup of military activity could be concealed from Cuban spies by better security than in Florida. The CIA had given a name to the staging ground. Launch Point Zebra would serve as the location from which the Miami Brigade was going to head for the Bay of Pigs.

Smith had completed his assignment to assist in the training of the brigade. He would be staying in Florida until the operation was declared over. Smith and Alverez shook hands as they would now part ways. Both men had come to respect each other after having worked side by side for two years. Leadership of the Miami Brigade now fell directly on Col. Alverez. He would no longer have to turn to Smith for anything. All of the weapons and supplies were being airlifted to Guatemala two days after the brigade arrived there. The CIA had used all of its political clout to obtain nine C-54 Skymasters. These were large four engine transports that could each carry nine tons of cargo or troops.

CHAPTER 6

LAUNCH POINT ZEBRA

KENNEDY WAS QUITE EAGER TO HEAR ABOUT THE PROGRESS OF OPER-
ation Zapata. He knew that in exactly thirty days the invasion
of Cuba would begin. All the troops, weapons and supplies
required for the overthrow of Castro had been airlifted to Guatemala. Agent Malone spoke with Kennedy as he held a thick
folder that contained all of the relevant information. The conversation was direct as neither man wanted to waste the others
time. Malone spoke first as he had the intelligence on the
staging ground that Kennedy wanted to know about:

"Launch Point Zebra is up and running as an operational
staging ground for the Miami Brigade. Guatemala is the perfect location to keep the unit for an entire month. As security
around the harbor is tight the chances of any information
leaking out to Castro or his spies is remote. Fort Owen was
not as isolated and thus did not provide a secret location for
the brigade. Launch Point Zebra is as designed a place where
the men can be kept until the operation begins. Even if Castro
knows that an invasion might take place he is unaware of our

timetable. I have more details about Launch Point Zebra in this folder. Now do you have any questions that I can answer about the staging ground?" Malone asked.

"No Agent Malone not at this time. I will of course want a full briefing on how Operation Zapata shall play out before it begins in mid-April." Kennedy replied.

"Yes of course Mr. President you just name the time and I will be here to explain the entire operation from start to finish as it has been planned." Malone confirmed.

"I want the briefing to take place on April 10th which gives you a month to trim down the content. Do not try to use complicated terms. Just make it so simple that a child could understand it. You are dismissed Agent Malone and thank you for the explanation of Launch Point Zebra as I found it very informative." Kennedy stated.

"Thank you sir, I will endeavor to be just as good with my next presentation." Malone insisted.

Malone calmly left the Oval Office as he had delivered the intelligence report as ordered. In addition he gave a very quick briefing to Kennedy on Launch Point Zebra. Malone over the course of several meetings developed a good dialogue with the president and was now looking forward to briefing him on April 10th. Kennedy still saw the CIA as not entirely on the level when it came to all the facts, but he trusted Malone. This basic level of trust was enough to allow the president to look upon the plan to invade Cuba as worthwhile and necessary. What had convinced Kennedy to go forward with Operation Zapata was Eisenhower endorsing the plan.

While they were both from different backgrounds and opposing political parties Kennedy held a great respect for Eisenhower. This respect came from the eight years that Ike had guided America from 1953 until 1961. Kennedy was determined to remove Castro from power by force and the Miami Brigade was the perfect tool to carry out this task. Limited involvement by the CIA was better than committing the US Army to an invasion of Cuba which would lead to heavy American casualities. There was also the Soviet Union's response which had to be taken into consideration.

Preventing Castro from turning Cuba into a military staging ground for the Soviet Union was at the top of Kennedy's goals with Operation Zapata. The entire western hemisphere needed to be free of any direct threat to America. If Castro was removed by force this action would send a strong message to the Soviet Union. Kennedy viewed his counterpart Khrushchev as being a man bent on expanding the power of Russia. To preserve the cold war the balance between the US and Russia had to be maintained. If Cuba was transformed into a missile launch platform it would upset the delicate balance between America and the Soviet Union. Kennedy was intent of solving a problem before it turned into a real threat to the United States.

Operation Zapata was soon to become a reality and the timing could not be better for Kennedy. He wished to show that his administration could be strong on foreign policy and deal with Castro. There were big questions hanging over the president about whether he would prove himself to be a powerful leader or merely a man who could talk tough. Operation Zapata could be used for political gain if it turned out as planned. Kennedy was still relying on the CIA to provide intelligence as the entire operation had been carried out by the agency. He vowed to never rely solely on the CIA for any future projects as it placed the president in a position of having to trust a group that was loose with the facts at times.

MARCH 17, 1961,
HAVANA, CUBA,
11:30 AM:

CASTRO AND CHE WERE INSPECTED A MILITIA UNIT THAT WAS STAtioned in the capital. They both arrived unannounced to ensure the men were not given time to prepare. Castro summoned the commander of the unit Lt. Gomez to give him a status report on the militia. Che watched as Castro spoke with the lieutenant:

"Comrade Gomez what is the strength of this militia and how many weapons does it have?" Castro asked.

"Sir this militia consists of a platoon of 40 men and there are 55 AK-47s for this platoon." Gomez answered.

"Very good lieutenant, now if the word came would your unit be prepared to fight?" Castro inquired.

"Yes sir, these men are prepared to give their lives to defend Cuba from any external threat." Gomez assured.

"Good, you may dismiss the men lieutenant. I believe that this militia is up to my high standards of excellence. I would like to inspect the barracks before heading out to the next militia." Castro stated.

"Wait one moment comrade; before we proceed to the barracks we should make certain that the assault rifles are in working order." Che insisted.

"Of course; lieutenant give me your rifle as I wish to test it to ensure it functions." Castro ordered.

"Yes sir, here is my rifle." Gomez remarked.

Castro looked over the AK-47 for a few seconds before aiming the weapon towards the sky and squeezing the trigger. This distinct sound of the assault rifle could be heard by everyone within a hundred yards. All of the rounds were fired before Castro lowered the weapon and returned it to Gomez. He smiled and nodded as the test had proven that the weapon was both clean and in good working order. Che motioned for another militiaman to hand over his AK-47 and the same test was repeated. Once again the weapon fired all of its rounds without incident and it was returned after Che confirmed that it worked as expected.

Castro led Gomez towards the barracks as he wanted to inspect the building to make sure that it was both clean and conformed to military regulations. Che remained outside with the men as he wanted to carefully inspect the uniforms before proceeding to the barracks. All of the members of the militia were dressed in olive shirts and pants. Che was impressed as none of boots were dirty and none of the clothes were wrinkled or dirty in any respect. He knew that not all militias were going to be as regulation as this one. It was a good start however to the inspection tour by Castro.

Gomez went through the barracks showing Castro the full tour of the facility. Everything inside the building was clean and placed neatly in its proper location. This impressed Castro further as there were some army units that did not look this well during inspection. Gomez was a commanding officer who took his job quite seriously as before Castro came to power he had been a mere sergeant under Batista. The rapid rise to lieutenant was enough to spur Gomez to hold his militia unit to a high standard of excellence.

Che entered the barracks and saw that Castro was speaking with Gomez towards the end of the building. He overheard the tail end of the conversation upon walking up to the two men:

"You have a fine militia here lieutenant. I am impressed with the level of discipline that everyone in the platoon follows. Take that as a direct complement on your skills as a leader. I want all of the militias in Cuba to be as good as this platoon." Castro observed.

With the inspection of the militia over Che wanted to speak to Castro about their next stop on the tour in the city of Castile. Gomez offered a quick salute and went outside to dismiss his platoon. Castro was eager to move on to Castile as he wanted to see if other militia units were up to the same high standard that had been seen at the one in Havana. There was a feeling of optimism by Castro as the first militia inspection had gone better than expected. Che viewed the militia in Havana as beyond a normal unit and did not expect the next one to be up to the same standard as the first.

Gomez and his platoon had proven to Castro that a well-disciplined militia was possible. It remained to be proven if more were going to be encountered during the rest of the inspection tour. Che viewed the militias as important, but only as an early warning unit that were used to delay the invaders until the Cuban Army could swing into action. Castro now saw militia units as a cheap way to supplement his military force. For the price of a few thousand AK-47s and a few months of training entire cities could be given limited protection.

MARCH 20, 1961, LPZ, GUATEMALA, 8:30 AM:

ALVEREZ AND THE MIAMI BRIGADE ARRIVED IN GUATEMALA WITH

their gear on schedule on March 2nd. They were keeping their skills sharp at Launch Point Zebra. All that the men could do was to train and wait. This predictable routine would not last more than a few weeks however as soon landing ships would appear in the harbor. These vessels would signal that Operation Zapata was getting close to its launch date. Alverez addressed the brigade as he wanted to raise their spirits:

"In less than a month this brigade shall begin an invasion of Cuba. Our goal is simple the removal of Castro and overthrow of his government. We have been provided all the weapons and supplies needed for this operation by the CIA. The burden to be successful in the invasion falls upon our shoulders once we are ashore. This brief time here in Guatemala is a chance for us to keep our skills sharp before the invasion begins. While I know that it is not the most exciting place to be we must focus on the task before us. I have managed to obtain a supply of several cases of tequila for us to enjoy. We shall toast to our invasion of Cuba and our removal of Castro. All of us have our reasons for wanting the dictator removed from power. In the end our efforts are justified as we wish to liberate Cuba from its current state. We shall save our people by force and write a new chapter in the history our nation. To success in the revolution! Down with Castro, long live Cuba!" Alverez shouted.

A loud cheer went out as the men raised their fists in support of what Alverez was saying. The tequila was then passed out to the members of the brigade and they each had two shots of the drink. This was an important moment of bonding for the brigade as their leader had to show that he cared for their emotional welfare. The need to keep the morale high was vital before the invasion began. Alverez would be relying on the men to carry out difficult jobs during the invasion. If spirits were low there was a danger of the members of the brigade losing focus during critical moments.

All of the tequila had been bought by Alverez as he felt the men required some downtime after all of the training and relocating they had been through. The colonel was proud of the members of the brigade and what they stood for. During his time serving Batista the Cuban Army had attempted to fight the growing insurgency. Soon the roles would be reversed as Alverez led an invasion force to start a revolution. This situation irony was not lost on Maj. Rodriquez as he spoke with Alverez about what they would soon be taking part in:

"We shall be going to Cuba as liberators, but is that not what Castro and his rebels claimed to be struggling for when they fought against Batista?" Rodriquez asked.

"Castro sought power for his own ends. It has always been the people of Cuba that have suffered. While there is no denying that Batista was corrupt, compared to the evils of Castro he was nothing. Being liberators has a different meaning to the Miami Brigade. These men are all exiles from Cuba and they want to return home to a land that is free. That freedom must be earned as right now it is Castro that rules our home." Alverez stated.

"Perhaps the term liberators is simply a way of saying that power can be turned for either good or evil. It just matters who wields the power. When Napoleon took power in France he liberated them from chaos which had raged for a bloody decade. When he invaded other lands he claimed to be liberating them. In reality he placed his will above the will of others." Rodriquez reflected.

"Freedom is a powerful light for which untold masses die in the dark." Alverez quoted.

"Who said that?" Rodriquez asked.

"I do not know, but the wording is exactly what poor Cuba has been through. Freedom is a goal that we all share for Cuba. We might not be as noble once power is in our hands, but hopefully our reign will be less bloody than that of Castro." Alverez replied.

Alverez was certain that a revolution in Cuba would bring about lasting change. Batista and Castro were perfect examples of what not to do as leaders. Peace and prosperity were more important to Alverez than the lust for power and control. He wanted to take Cuba in a more democratic direction. For America and many counties in Western Europe the legacy of democracy was a positive one which transformed these nations. Alverez wished for Cuba to enjoy the fruits of democracy as well. In many ways the colonel wanted to emulate George Washington.

Rodriquez was looking forward to the revolution as he wanted to enhance his status to something higher than being a major. As history showed those who succeeded as leaders of revolutions normally became the leaders of the nations they had liberated. Alverez and Rodriquez were both trusted by the members of the brigade. They could have great influence in shaping a new government once Castro was removed. These were issues that could be settled once the invasion had proven successful. Until then the focus needed to remain on getting ashore and starting a revolution.

MARCH 25, 1961,
HOUSTON, TX,
9:30 AM:

AGENT MALONE HAD COME TO HOUSTON TO SIGN OFF ON THE PAPER-work for two LSTs (Landing Ship Tank). These ships would deliver the members of the Miami Brigade to the Bay of Pigs beaches. In addition there would be several destroyers, an oil tanker and a freighter. These ships were all to sail to Cuba on the night of April 16th with the small squadron reaching the Bay of Pigs on the morning of the 17th for the invasion. Malone would be taking possession of the LSTs from the US Navy and was required to sign off on the paperwork. It was a task which normally could have been done be a lowly clerk.

As the CIA wanted to show that it was acting in good faith it had dispatched the senior agent in charge of the operation. Upon reaching the front office for the small naval depot Malone was greeted by Capt. Stanza and handed the forms to fill out granting the CIA use and ownership of the vessels. The US Navy would provide the other ships on a temporary basis for the duration of the invasion. Capt. Stanza showed Malone the two LSTs and stated that both had served in World War II. This fact reminded the CIA agent of just how old these ships really were. The defenses on the LSTs were a pair of machineguns at the bow and stern.

After seeing that the LSTs were capable of carrying out the

task they were slated for Malone signed off on the transfer orders. Stanza discussed the use of the ships which Malone managed to downplay for reasons of security about Operation Zapata:

"These two landing ships will provide the CIA with the ability to land troops and vehicles ashore. What are you planning to do with them?" Stanza asked bluntly.

"An exercise to test military effectiveness is required and the CIA wishes to make absolutely certain that no bias from the US Navy is involved." Malone replied.

"I guess that makes sense, but it sure is a lot of trouble to take these two LSTs off our hands." Stanza added.

"The CIA has many projects on its hands and they are all very important. We are the foreign intelligence branch of the US Government. That is all you need to know about what we do." Malone stressed.

"Whatever, the ships are yours now." Stanza confirmed.

"Good they shall be put to excellent use." Malone added.

With the two LSTs now obtained the CIA would send both of the ships to Guatemala. Launch Point Zebra was about to receive its two most important vessels. Malone was pleased with the swift transfer of the ships had not taken up too much of his time. He took one more glance at the vessels before heading to the airport to fly back to Langley. The orders that were signed by the CIA agent instructed the ships to report to Launch Point Zebra by no later than April 10th. The crews for the LSTs were already lined up. Malone would place a call and in a few hours the ships would be underway.

MARCH 28, 1961,
THE WHITE HOUSE,
10:30 AM:

PRESIDENT KENNEDY STOOD OVER A SMALL MOCKUP OF THE BAY OF Pigs and asked McNamara to play out the first stages of the invasion. Small model planes and ships would stand in for the real versions on the mockup as Kennedy watched and listened. McNamara explained how the invasion would play out:

"At 5:00 AM eight A-26s attack three Cuban airfields where their entire air force is stationed. As it will be too dark for anti-aircraft guns to get a clear shot the crews of the planes should be relatively safe. Once the aircraft have strafed the airfields they will proceed southeast to the Bay of Pigs. At 6:45 AM the LSTs will be unloading the members of the Miami Brigade on the beach. This is the most vital part of the invasion. If the brigade can get ashore without be opposing they stand a good chance of moving inland and starting a revolution. As you know if anything goes wrong during the landing an evacuation from the beach would prove to be a disaster for both the men and the entire operation. There are several towns that are near to the Bay of Pigs that can be captured by the Miami Brigade. This will provide a foothold for the men to spread further inland. Getting the people of Cuba to rise up in revolution is the most important part of the invasion after the landing. A force of 1,400 men needs to grow to stand any chance against Castro's regime. The LSTs are heading to Guatemala and each of them shall carry 700 troops. They have been repainted to remove any US markings." McNamara explained.

"Agent Malone will give me the same briefing in just over a week from now. I wanted to hear the facts before he presents his description of events. This will be the first military operation of my time as president. It might be a wonderful success or an utter failure. The CIA has run this plan from start to finish and I have placed my faith in that plan. We shall see if they thought this entire project through to the last detail." Kennedy remarked.

"The CIA and its agents are just as fallible as any other part of the US Government. They might work in the world of shadows, but that does not make them better than the rest of us humans." McNamara assured.

Kennedy took McNamara at his word and smiled as he studied the mockup of the Bay of Pigs beach intensely. The Miami Brigade was at the staging ground and the eight A-26s were stationed in Florida. All of the pieces were in place for the invasion. Operation Zapata was moving towards its starting time as April 17th neared. The CIA was sending intelligence reports on a weekly basis to the White House. Kennedy and McNamara were eager to hear anything about Castro. Both Che and Raul were also mentioned in the reports as they held senior positions in Cuba. Most of the intelligence was routine, but Kennedy wanted to know about even the mundane facts as they might prove important.

Operation Zapata and its implications were mentioned so often in the White House that Kennedy had to tell his staff to let the matter rest. The president accepted full responsibility for the project and its outcome. He had other matters that required his attention and energies. Cuba was important, but it had grown out of proportion to the efforts being directed against Castro. Kennedy wanted a single day to pass without talking about the looming Operation Zapata. He was grateful the project would begin in less than a month. Having to read through endless intelligence reports had taken its toll on the president's stress level.

While the CIA was providing plenty of information on Castro and his ties with the Soviet Union much of it was repeating earlier reports. Kennedy began to stack up all of the red folders and casually look through them once a week instead of every day. Operation Zapata briefings gained more attention from the president. He foresaw a new era with Cuba if all turned out well. Hopes were high by the Kennedy Administration that their first foreign operation would turn out successful as it could pave the way for future projects.

APRIL 5, 1961, HAVANA, CUBA, 2:00 PM:

CASTRO AND CHE HAD BY NOW BOTH INSPECTED THE MILITIAS IN every major city in Cuba. While some were in perfect shape others needed vast improvements. Overall Castro was satisfied that the militias were a good idea, but they needed to be all be brought up to a high standard that was set by the first one visited in Havana. Che was also impressed for the most part with the militias. Still there were several militias that had to be developed further before Castro or Che would view them as competent. Castro spoke with Che about the inspection tour and his views on the militias:

"We have returned to Havana after spending over a week looking over the militias. I am glad to finally be back as viewing all of those barracks and men was a tiring affair that in the future shall be carried out by Raul or one of my senior generals. My rightful place is here in Havana where I can lead this government. A commander must never get down in the trenches too often. Still I thank you for suggesting the armed militia concept to me as it might prove invaluable. The Cuban Army might need assistance against enemy invaders." Castro remarked.

"I enjoyed the tour of all the militias, Havana is only one part of Cuba and getting away from the capital is nice to do every now and then." Che stated.

"Next time there is an inspection of the militias that is needed perhaps I will send you. Havana has all of the comforts of home for me. Spending time in the middle of the jungle is not fun when you do it for more than two days in a row. Being a rebel was an exciting part of my life, but I am glad it is over." Castro admitted.

"Havana does offer things that most cities in Cuba lack; still I often feel the need to stretch my legs." Che added.

"I know that you really want to start your revolutions in South America, but wait until the end of the year before leaving. Kennedy might prove to be my most capable opponent yet. Eisenhower was smart, but too old while Kennedy is young and full of passion." Castro observed.

"Alright, I will stay in Cuba until the end of the year if nothing has happened then it will be time to leave. My desire to spread revolution across South America is a passion that I must follow to wherever it leads. Cuba was only the beginning of what could be an entire group of South American nations aligned with the Soviet Union. That is my goal and my vision." Che confirmed.

"Patience, you shall get your chance. Just stick with me for the rest of this year." Castro repeated.

Castro viewed Che as his right hand man and desired that he stay in Cuba until the end of the year. If nothing had occurred between the United States and Cuba by the end of 1961 than it was likely that Kennedy would not attempt any serious action during his first term. Che was still enjoying the delights of Cuba, but his extended stay had become somewhat dull. Fighting beside Castro as a rebel were days long gone. Che desired action as sitting still did not fit his personality style. Castro understood this quality in Che as it was impossible to ignore. Even so the Cuban leader wanted to get to the end of 1961 before turning Che loose.

APRIL 16, 1961,
LPZ, GUATEMALA
6:00 AM:

IN A FEW HOURS THE LSTs WOULD BE LOADED WITH SUPPLIES AND the members of the Miami Brigade. They would set sail for Cuba before noon to reach the Bay of Pigs beach around 6:45 AM. Col. Alverez had decided that one last speech to the Miami Brigade was in order. He stood in front of the formation with Maj. Rodriquez at his side. Appealing to the passion that drove each of the Cubans Alverez kept his speech short and to the point:

"Tomorrow we land at the Bay of Pigs in Cuba and it shall be our finest hour. We have trained for this moment and it will soon be upon us. Castro has turned our home into a land of fear and tyranny. Our job is to reverse that situation by force. A violent revolution against Castro is our main goal. Fighting for freedom is a noble goal and each of us is about to undertake that task. I wish you all good luck as no matter what happens we shall need it in our mission. May God go with us and may he grant us the strength to tear down Castro's regime. That is all you are dismissed." Alverez announced.

Alverez spoke from the heart and did not attempt to sugar-coat the situation. He was aware of the risks and the obstacles to the operation. Even so there was a strong feeling of destiny among the men of the brigade. Both Alverez and Rodriquez shared these feelings to a certain degree though less than the rank and file. After living in America for several years all of the men were eager to be going back to Cuba. They understood that force would be required to make their stay permanent. Alverez had hoped for this day even since Batista was forced from power over two years earlier.

Morale among the Miami Brigade was high as they waited to board the LSTs. Hopes of overthrowing Castro were to be found among most of the men in the brigade. Their moment of glory was finally just a few hours away and all of them were looking forward to the invasion. A hearty breakfast with a shot of tequila helped boost the mood among all the men. Normally alcohol was not served, but Alverez saw little harm in the men being in good spirits with a single shot of tequila.

President Kennedy had sent a message of good luck to the members of the Miami Brigade and it would be read to the men once the ships had set sail. Agent Smith and Agent Malone had also sent a message to wish the men of the Miami Brigade well in their operation. The crews of the A-26s were sent similar messages of good luck as they would be the first to fly in harm's way. With all of the pieces now in position Operation Zapata would begin early on April 17th. Castro and Che were vaguely aware that the United States might attempt something, but had no idea of the time or scope of the threat.

CHAPTER 7

THE BAY OF PIGS

APRIL 17, 1961,
2 MILES NORTH OF CUBA,
5:30 AM:

EIGHT A-26S FLEW TOWARDS THREE AIRFIELDS NEAR HAVANA WITH orders to destroy the enemy air force on the ground before heading to the Bay of Pigs. All of the American planes flew at 200 feet and their flight crews maintained radio silence. Operation Zapata was underway and soon the calm morning would turn into a violent maelstrom. All of the A-26s were given a specific airfield to strafe with the main airfield in Havana being assigned to four of the planes. The other two airfields near the capital of Cuba would each be strafed by a pair of A-26s. Flying low under Cuban radar the planes were not detected until they were nearly over the airfields.

Each of the planes were carrying eight 2.5 inch rockets and 2,400 rounds of ammo for their guns. This amount of firepower was more than enough to strafe the airfields if all the targets were out in the open. As the first rays of sunlight broke over the horizon the A-26s split up and headed for their designated targets. The flight crews all knew that from this point forward they were in danger of being shot down. The three airfields near Havana now began to scramble pilots towards their planes. It was too late however as the A-26s opened fire before the Cubans could even start their aircraft engines.

As the planes flew in very low the Cuban antiaircraft gunners were unable to get a good lead on the A-26s and fired off rounds that missed the targets by several dozen feet. The strafing runs were quite successful as nearly all of the Cuban planes were destroyed on the ground. Two Cuban planes did survive as a T-33 jet trainer and British Sea Fury prop attack plane were in a hardened hanger at one of the airfields. These surviving aircraft was readied for takeoff, but the damaged runway would have to be repaired first. Several rockets had struck the concrete making any takeoff impossible until the holes were filled in and smoothed over.

2 MINUTES LATER:

HAVING COMPLETED THEIR STRAFING RUNS AND WITH THE SUN steadily coming up by the minute the A-26s headed for the Bay of Pigs to the southeast. They had destroyed most of the Cuban Air Force, but had missed two planes which were still grounded due to a damaged runway. In a little over an hour the Miami Brigade would be landing at the beaches in southeastern Cuba. Providing air cover for the LSTs was now the only task left for the A-26s to carry out before they headed for Honduras. With the strafing of the airfields the Cubans were now aware that something was happening. Castro and Che were alerted of the attacks and they placed the military forces on high alert all over the nation.

THE BAY OF PIGS,
VERDE BEACH,
6:45 AM:

COL. ALVEREZ COCKED HIS M1 CARBINE AND MOTIONED FOR THE MEN behind him to do the same with their weapons. Soon the bow doors would open and the LST would come to a stop on Verde Beach. The LSTs were built to run themselves aground without damaging the ships. The LSTs were now in position to unload their human cargo on the beach. The bow doors opened and the members of Miami Brigade stepped out into the chest high water to wade ashore. Col. Alverez was the first member of the brigade to reach the beach and there was silence as no Cuban forces were present to oppose the landing. It was a mild surprise to the men as they expected some form of enemy opposition.

In the skies over the beach eight A-26s could be seen flying in large circles to provide air cover. Once the men were ashore the supplies would follow in a process that was going to take an entire hour. This stage of invasion would place the Miami Brigade in the greatest amount of danger. Without the supplies the entire force would grind to a halt as ammo, food and water ran out. The freighter was carrying all of the supplies for the Miami Brigade as there had been no more room on the LSTs. The freighter was modern and had been built in the mid-1950s unlike the rest of the ships which all came from World War II. Once the two LSTs were finished unloading their human cargo the freighter would move begin sending small boats of supplies ashore.

Radio contact was established between the A-26s and the men of Miami Brigade. Just as Alverez asked about the strafing runs on the airfields two planes were seen coming towards the beach. The T-33 and Sea Fury were both painted with Cuban Air Force markings. Armed with rockets and machineguns the Cuban planes headed directly for the freighter and began to strafe the vessel. On the first pass the Cuban planes managed to cripple the freighter and soon after the ship began to sink. Only half of the supplies had reached the beach while the rest including the radios went down with the freighter. Now the A-26s became the next target of the Cuban planes.

Flying over 200 mph faster than the American planes the Cuban T-33 could pick off its targets at will. Two of the A-26s were hit forcing them to crash in the jungle just beyond Verde Beach. Both flight crews were killed and the rest of the A-26s were compelled to head for Honduras at once. With their air cover gone the men of the Miami Brigade were now on their own. Alverez ordered the men into the jungle to avoid being strafed. It was a prudent move as the Cuban planes still had ammo for their guns.

With only half of their needed supplies the members of the Miami Brigade headed into the jungle as fast as their legs would carry them. Alverez wanted to capture two small towns close to Verde Beach. Hiding in the jungle was not what the Miami Brigade had come to Cuba for. Alverez motioned for Rodriquez to speak with him as he wanted to know the current status of their supplies:

"Major how much of the supplies did we lose when the freighter went down?" Alverez asked.

"Half of our food, water and ammo have been lost as well as all of the radios. Most of the crew were killed and a handful managed to swim ashore. This brigade is in serious trouble." Rodriquez replied.

"I am aware of the situation, but we have no choice other than pressing forward with the plan. Both of the LSTs have left the area and that means there is no going back for any of us. We have a job to do and that means that we push forward with our goal of starting a revolution against Castro." Alverez observed.

"Yes colonel, I will get the men ready to move out as we need to move fast to capture those towns. If a revolution is to be started we are going to need support from the local populations." Rodriquez stated.

With the Cuban planes now gone it was safe for the men of the Miami Brigade to move out. Alverez wanted to capture the towns as a way of boosting morale which needed improvement at this point. Surging forward the men rushed out the jungle near Cortez and Ortiz. Both the towns had only a handful of militia stationed in each of them. Alverez gave the order to advance and soon the towns were in the hands of the Miami Brigade. These small victories were a start for the men, but larger cities would need to be captured. In addition the people of Cuba had to be convinced to join the revolution as their support was vital to defeating Castro.

Cortez and Ortiz were small towns of only 500 people as the Bay of Pigs was a fishing location. Alverez hoped to gather support from the towns, but none of the people were willing to join the invaders. Loyalty to Castro and Cuba was too strong. Alverez ordered that a defensive perimeter be setup around the towns. Any advance to capture other towns was going to require the efforts of the entire brigade. With half of the supplies available any fighting with the Cuban Army would prove to be a one sided battle. Alverez focused on capturing more towns and hopefully convincing Cubans to join the brigade in a revolution. Speed was critical as soon the Cuban Army would be alerted to the invaders.

HAVANA, CUBA, 15 MINUTES LATER:

NEWS OF THE INVASION HAD NOT REACHED CASTRO AND CHE AS THEY were discussing economic programs to stimulate the Cuban workers. All of these programs were approved of by the Soviet Union and were tried socialist plans that collectivized a nation. There was a relaxed atmosphere in the room until the wooden door swung open with such force that both men turned to see who was disturbing their polite conversation. A messenger came running into the room where Castro and Che were talking. He saluted and then informed the two men of his message:

"An invasion of Cuba is taking place at the Bay of Pigs! Two of our planes drove off American planes and sank a freighter before returning to their airbase! Both pilots reported that a force over 1,000 has landed! What are your orders?" The messenger inquired.

"Mobilize all nearby militia to the Bay of Pigs area. The Cuban Army must also converge on that part to contain and then wipe out the invaders." Castro ordered.

"Yes sir." The messenger confirmed.

"It would appear that President Kennedy has decided to take action against Cuba. The United States is no doubt behind this invasion. We must crush it quickly before it has a chance to grow in size and strength." Che insisted.

"Naturally, I am going to the Bay of Pigs to take charge

of the situation. Leaving this to the generals is too much of a risk. This is a problem that must be dealt with by the leader of Cuba." Castro added.

"That is a wise move. Your very presence will inspire the men to fight harder." Che remarked.

"Come, your assistance shall be needed as putting down an enemy invasion requires plenty of leadership and you have that in abundance comrade." Castro ordered.

"Kennedy is daring, but his plan shall fail as the people of Cuba will protect you." Che commented.

"The people of Cuba will fight to the death to save this nation from those evil capitalist pigs." Castro vowed.

Castro and Che were surprised only the by timing of the invasion as they believed that Kennedy would have waited at least six months before attempt such a daring operation. The two men headed for the Bay of Pigs as they wished to be in the center of the action. The Cuban Army and militia units were both mobilized. Soon the invaders were going to be facing thousands of armed men intent on their destruction. Castro and Che headed for the airport as they had a private plane for their own use as senior leaders in the government. Reaching the Bay of Pigs quickly was all that mattered to Castro and Che as they wanted to assume command of all Cuban forces opposing the invaders.

As Castro got in the backseat of the car he lit a cigar and smiled. The waiting for a possible invasion had finally come to an end. In a way the Cuban leader was relieved to be able to face a direct threat. It reminded Castro of the irony that he had once been a rebel trying to keep a revolution alive. Kennedy had proven to be more daring in months than Eisenhower was in nearly two years of planning. Che and Castro were both eager to defeat the invaders and show that Cuba could defend itself for US interference.

While Castro and Che believed the invaders would be defeated they were not taking any chances. A large part of the Cuban Army would be sent to oppose the enemy in addition to the militias. Castro radioed the local militia commanders to the north of the Bay of Pigs. He ordered them to mobilize their force and quickly head towards the invading force. Stopping the enemy from advancing further was Castro's main objective at the moment. If the invaders could be contained their force might be quickly defeated by the Cuban Army. Che believed that it might take longer to defeat the invaders as they were probably trained by the CIA in guerrilla battle tactics.

ORTIZ, CUBA, 30 MINUTES LATER:

ALVEREZ WANTED TO KEEP THE MOMENTUM OF THE INVASION GOING. He ordered the brigade to head north towards the city of Palpite at a quick pace of double time. If Palpite could be captured it would provide the invaders with access to both food and the armory of the city. Having a desperate need for supplies and ammo, Alverez was compelled to remedy the situation before it got any worse for the men of the brigade. As the men began to march forward they encountered Cuban militia units that opened fire seconds later. Alverez ordered the brigade to form a defensive half circle as reaching Palpite was now an impossible task. Survival had just become the top priority of the brigade.

Although the Miami Brigade had enough firepower to deal with the militias moving forward would expose the men to the enemy. Holding their position was the only real option for Alverez. Retreat was out of the question as the brigade had to prevail or die. For the moment the men of the Miami Brigade held the advantage. Alverez passed the word along that every man was to hold his ground no matter what. At this point the militias were unable to drive back the brigade. However additional militias were converging on Ortiz. The situation was a stalemate for the time being as advance and retreat were both out of the question for the brigade.

A new threat to the brigade was heard in the distance as a T-34 tank started to approach Ortiz. With only five bazooka rounds among their supplies every shot needed to count. Taking out the enemy tank was imperative as the firepower on the armored machine was enough to wipe out most of the brigade.

Alverez ordered for the bazooka to the loaded and fired. It was the most obvious order in the world as the Cuban tank continued to close towards Ortiz. Seconds later the bazooka fired and it managed to destroy the turret of the T-34. A black cloud of smoke confirmed the bazooka had done its job and saved the brigade from a world of hurt.

Alverez ordered the men to dig in as they were going to remain at Ortiz for as long as their supplies held out. Advancing forward would expose the brigade to enemy fire and allow the Cuban Army to surround it. Staying put would permit the Miami Brigade to defend itself for hours if not days in its current position. Alverez now realized that the revolution would not take place and that he could only delay the defeat of the brigade. Causalities suffered by the Miami Brigade so far were light, but this was expected to change in the near future. Three men had already been killed; however Alverez knew that this was just the beginning of the death toll.

Morale among the Miami Brigade began to decline as the men came to the realization that the revolution was no longer possible. Even so the desire to stay alive kept their fighting spirits up. Both Alverez and Rodriquez walked among the men to show that the officers would not abandon them. It was an important move as the men had to see that their superiors cared about them. Holding the defensive line around Ortiz was a simple task for the moment. The Miami Brigade still had the numbers and firepower on its side. This military equation was rapidly changing however with each passing minute. Militias were continuing to pour into the area. The chance to fight the invaders spurred the Cubans on towards Ortiz with an intense zeal in their bellies.

Alverez wanted to hold out as long as possible as surrender did not enter into his mind at this point. The situation for the Miami Brigade was serious, but not yet desperate. Running up the white flag seemed premature at this time. Even so the endgame for the Miami Brigade had changed from victory to either surrender or total defeat. This grim reality was impossible for Alverez or Rodriquez to ignore. As for the men of the brigade they were too focused on fighting to worry about the fate of the unit. More tanks could be heard in the distance and soon the bazooka rounds would be depleted as most of the antitank ammunition had sunk with the freighter.

Alverez ordered the bazooka man to fire only when he had a clear shot and not to miss. It was a restatement of the obvious instructions given to him the first time a tank had threatened the brigade. Alverez knew that tanks were the biggest threat to his men. The jungle would provide cover against any aerial threat. With no armor of their own the Miami Brigade could only fight troops as they would be obliterated if faced with scores of tanks or armored vehicles. Having four rounds left to deal with tanks made the situation grow somewhat more perilous for the men of Miami Brigade.

3 MILES NORTH OF ORTIZ, 2 HOURS LATER:

CASTRO AND CHE HAD LANDED AT AN AIRPORT ONLY A FEW MILES from Ortiz. A temporary command post was setup for the Cuban Army in a former church. Castro spoke with Gen. Gomez of the Cuban Army about the progress against the enemy invaders:

"Here is a map of the area and here is the Cuban Army along with the militia units. The enemy brigade is here holding the town of Ortiz. They have created a defensive line and our attempts to breach it each ended in failure. I believe that more men should solve the problem and give us the victory over these invaders. I am preparing to send an entire division against the enemy." Gomez explained.

"General the problem is not manpower, but firepower. Sending in more troops towards the enemy position will only increase the number of targets that the enemy can shoot at. We have tanks while the enemy does not and these tanks must be used to greater effect compared to sending them in one at a time with no infantry support. Order six tanks to assault the enemy position and have troops follow close behind to support the tanks. Once these invaders have been dealt with your days as a general are over. Such incompetence is not acceptable under my command. The fact that you have not prevailed over this enemy force tells me that something is wrong with your military thinking. You have managed to rise to the rank of general, but your skills as a military leader are severely lacking. Now carry out my orders at once and from this point forward you report to me. All of your authority is hereby suspended. You will remain here to ensure that my orders are carried out." Castro ordered.

"Yes sir." Gomez acknowledged.

Castro had relieved Gomez on the spot for the good of the Cuban Army. He could not afford to have a general who lacked the basic understanding of military tactics and strategy. Defeating the invaders was too important a task for the Cuban Army to mess up. Che stood silently next to Castro as now was not the time to voice his own opinion on the situation. He was there to support Castro in whatever capacity required. Che understood the value of keeping quiet at certain times. Now was just such an occasion for silence to prevail.

Castro was confident that the enemy invaders could be defeated in a short time if the Cuban Army and militias were thrown into battle behind tanks. This combination was more than the invaders could handle as they had no tanks or artil-lery to oppose the Cubans. Hoping for a quick victory Castro was placing his faith in a sound military tactic of overwhelming firepower. As long as the tanks were not destroyed the invaders would soon be forced to surrender or die where they stood. Che took notes as he wanted to appear useful at this critical stage of the decision making.

Gomez followed Castro's orders and began plotting on how to survive the months ahead. It was well known that anyone who displeased Castro in any manner ended up dead or in prison for the rest of their life. Gomez knew that his career in the Cuban Army was over and that if he did not act fast his life might also be coming to a sudden end in a violent manner. There were only two options for Gomez to consider. Escape from Cuba or ask for mercy from Castro for his failure. As Gomez did not trust in Castro to show mercy he began considering escape from Cuba. At the moment the defeat of the invaders was all that Gomez needed to worry about. Castro would not have the general arrested until after the battle.

ALVEREZ CAREFULLY LOOKED THROUGH A PAIR OF BINOCULARS AND SAW that six T-34s were heading straight for Ortiz with a large formation of Cuban troops behind them. Dealing with the enemy tanks would require all four of the remaining bazooka rounds and some kind of military miracle for the other two. Alverez ordered two teams of men to race towards the remaining tanks once the first four were destroyed. Armed with grenades these men were to throw the grenades at the treads. It was a risky move as if the men were spotted they would be killed by the tank's machinegun. Rodriquez took charge of one of the teams and waited for the bazooka to take out the first four tanks.

With quick loading and firing the bazooka man took out four of the six T-34 tanks. This left two that had to be dealt with. Even if all the tanks were destroyed the Cuban infantry also needed to be repulsed. Alverez gave the order for the men to rush to remaining tanks. In a moment of pure courage Rodriquez took off with the grenades and raced around to the side of one of the tanks. The major threw a batch of four grenades at one of the T-34s before dropping to the ground. A deafening explosive was seen seconds later as the grenades blew off a track on the tank bringing it to a sudden halt.

Maj. Rodriquez now urged all of the men who had come with him to return to the defensive line. He took out his Colt .45 automatic pistol and quickly charged at the remaining T-34. Seconds later there was another explosion as Rodriquez had thrown five grenades at the track of the last tank. Although the T-34 was quickly immobilized, Rodriquez died from shrapnel wounds during the blast. With the exception of the major none of the other members of the Miami Brigade were killed during the attack on the tanks. Alverez now ordered the men to open fire on the Cuban infantry. Having no tanks to shield them from the incoming fire the Cuban troops were unable to drive the invaders back.

Despite the success by the Miami Brigade at taking care of the tanks and repelling the troops they were beginning to run low on ammo. Another large scale attack by the Cuban Army would quickly deplete all of the ammo that the brigade had left. Alverez planned on pulling the men back the next time they were attacked by the Cubans. The jungle was less than a hundred yards behind the Miami Brigade. This would be the perfect location to seek shelter as no enemy tanks could pursue through the thick clusters of trees. Alverez seeing that the Cubans were out of sight for the moment ordered that Rodriquez's body be recovered. It was important for the morale of the brigade that the major be retrieved.

3 MILES NORTH OF ORTIZ,
15 MINUTES LATER:

CASTRO WAS IMPRESSED BY THE INVADERS ABILITY TO HOLD OUT against a combined tank and infantry assault on their position. Still they needed to be defeated no matter what the cost. Another Cuban assault with tanks and infantry would likely break the defensive line the defenders were holding. Castro this time was taking no chances as he ordered 12 T-34s and 5,000 Cuban soldiers to assault the invaders. This was a force twice the size of the first one that had been sent out. Che and Gomez both nodded in approval of the decision. Castro wanted to bring a swift end to the battle and sending in a large force was the best way to bring about this goal.

Gomez sent the order out as he wanted to show that he was cooperating to the fullest extent. Castro was only paying attention the battle and his plans for dealing with the general would have to wait. Che had come along to accompany Castro out of a request and now was bored as he strongly wished to take part in the action. Grabbing a pair of binoculars and informing Castro of his action Che headed outside. The sight of tanks and troops mustering for battle greeted him. Wanting to see the invaders with his very eyes Che climbed aboard one of the T-34s and ordered the commander to head south.

Knowing that Che was a senior leader in Cuba the tank commander obeyed the order at once. The other T-34s followed behind the lead tank along with the soldiers as the formation headed out. Che was excited to be finally taking part in some action. Castro spoke with him over the radio:

"Are you sure that taking part in this assault will satisfy your desire for combat?" Castro asked bluntly.

"Yes comrade, I have been feeling the need to fight off the invaders ever since they arrived in Cuba. It reminds me of being a warrior for our great cause of socialism. This is the most passionate act for a revolutionary like myself to partake in." Che confirmed.

"Very well enjoy yourself, but you come back alive as the revolutions in South America still await. Crush these invaders and achieve victory." Castro added.

"I will do my best." Che promised.

"Good luck comrade." Castro added.

Che would man the DSK-12 machinegun on the top of the T-34. He was more than ready to engage in combat with the invaders. Unlike Castro the need for adventure was hardly quenched for Che. Fighting was one of the few activities that made him feel at peace. As the tanks headed south Che smiled as he calmly sat on the top of the turret awaiting battle. Morale among the Cubans was high as they believed the invaders would soon be crushed. Castro's presence near the battle was enough to encourage the soldiers to fight harder. Che coming along also raised the morale of the men even higher.

The lead tank commander knew that keeping Che alive was also a priority for him. Castro would punish anyone who allowed Che to get killed. This fact forced the tank commander to be careful in his advance. With less than two miles to go the Cuban force was heading towards the invaders at a speed of seven miles per hour. For all of the soldiers this was a fast march, but nothing to strain their bodies to the point of exhaustion. Che looked through his binoculars and saw Ortiz in the distance. Breaking the enemy position would require both speed and constant pressure by the Cuban force. Castro had given strict orders that all forces were to advance. As long as the tanks were not destroyed the Cuban soldiers would be safe from enemy fire.

Che saw some of the invaders getting ready to oppose the Cuban force. He was impressed with their tactics so far and felt a slight amount of admiration for them. This feeling was quickly replaced by the desire to crush all of the invaders. Cuba had to be protected from anyone who attempted to upset the government. Castro was the leader and socialism followed as the ideology. While all of the invaders might be brave they were fighting to destroy the system that Castro and Che had installed in Cuba. This clash was between two ideologies as much as two armies as America and Cuba were too different to see eye to eye on any issue. Che cocked the machinegun and waited for the tank to get within 200 yards of the invaders.

CHAPTER 8

FIGHT OR SURRENDER

ONE DAY AFTER COMING ASHORE THE MIAMI BRIGADE WAS HOLDING ON by its fingernails against the Cuban Army and the militias. Alverez and the men of the brigade had been forced to retreat from Ortiz. They were now in the jungle 500 yards from the Bay of Pigs. Several dozen causalities had been sustained by the Miami Brigade during the previous day's fighting. Even so the Cubans had failed in two assaults. Alverez knew that time was not on his side. Fighting against the Cuban Army would be an impossible task. Delaying a final choice between continuing fighting or surrendering was all that Alverez could look forward to.

With the death of Maj. Rodriquez the morale of the Miami Brigade was in dire straits. Fighting for survival was the only thing that kept the men with any sense of military discipline. Alverez could only do so much to raise the spirits of the men. Staying in the jungle was not improving the mood of the Miami Brigade. There were annoying bugs and snakes along with the humidity. All of these factors created a draining experience for anyone who stayed in the jungle more than a few hours. For the moment the Miami Brigade was not under direct threat, but Alverez predicted the Cuban Army would attempt to drive the brigade back to Verde Beach.

As if the situation was not bad enough for Alverez and the men the meager supplies were nearly exhausted due to the ongoing fighting. Each member of the brigade was ordered to ration his ammunition as much as possible. Alverez predicted that in less than a day all of the ammo would be entirely gone. Without ammo the brigade was no longer a fighting force. Alverez gave the command that any Cuban killed was to be stripped of anything he carried on his person. Fighting in the jungle prevented the Cuban Army from quickly surrounding the men of the Miami Brigade. Stealing supplies from dead soldiers was possible among the trees.

Col. Alverez spoke with Capt. Vista as he was now the second highest ranking officer in the brigade. The entire conversation was brief and to the point:

"We must hold our position as if the Cuban Army drives us back to Verde Beach the entire Miami Brigade shall be encircled and wiped out." Alverez explained.

"Yes sir, our resistance in this jungle must be as tough as we can make it on the Cuban Army. However in the end there are only two options to select from. We can either continue to fight or surrender. As our supplies continue to dwindle our situation becomes graver. I know that you do not want to hear this, but surrendering is the only way to save the lives of the men. They are prepared to die and that is enough to satisfy our honor. This revolution failed within the first hours after the invasion began. All of us are fighting for a goal that is only a dream instead of a possible reality." Vista added.

"Yes, I get your point captain. As commander of this brigade the decision is mine to make however. When the time comes to surrender I shall give the order and then the Miami Brigade will be no more." Alverez stressed.

CASTRO AND HIS MILITARY STAFF WERE NOW IN ORTIZ AS THE invaders had been forced back into the jungle. Che was eager to pursue the enemy, but among the trees the tanks and air power were useless. This meant the fighting was going to be determined by sheer manpower. Sending in waves of Cuban troops was a simple enough tactic as Castro wanted the invaders to suffer heavy losses which would compel them to withdraw further. This time Che was going to remain with Castro as sending him into the jungle would be too risky. He survived the previous assault by sitting in a tank most of the time.

This first wave of Cuban soldiers was ordered to assault the invaders at once. They were to scout out the enemy position and determine any weak points. These were straightforward orders to obey and to lead the men Gen. Gomez had been selected by Castro. By placing a general in charge of the assault it would show all the Cuban soldiers that no one was above risky operations. There was a second reason as Gomez had fallen out of favor with Castro and the dictator wanted the general to be exposed to as much danger as possible. Gomez had been planning to escape from Cuba. Now his only destination would be the jungle to the south of Ortiz.

With hopes of a quick victory over the invaders now gone a forced retreat and surrender of the enemy was the next best option for Castro. If the invaders surrendered the entire failed invasion could be used as a propaganda triumph. Gomez had been ordered to drive the invaders out of the jungle, but even Castro expected this goal to require several attempts. If Gomez was killed than it would save Castro from having to arrest the general once the invaders had been defeated. Che watched as Gomez went outside to take command of the Cuban troops. The general seemed to be in good spirits. Castro then turned to Che and discussed the need to drive the invaders back:

"Gomez will attempt to find a weak point in the defenses of the invaders. If they can be pushed back with relative ease

I shall order additional troops forward. The enemy has limited supplies and will not be able to hold out for more than a few days at most. Once enough pressure is applied it should compel a retreat by the invaders. The jungle is the only thing preventing the Cuban Army from surrounding these invaders." Castro explained.

"Victory over the enemy is simply a matter of time they are outnumbered and outgunned. When the moment of triumph arrives we shall both celebrate." Che stated.

"One step at a time, the invaders seem to be led by a clever commander. He has made few mistakes and this is the only reason they have not been defeated yet. Gomez might have wasted countless Cuban soldiers if I did not come out here to take charge of the situation. Generals are supposed to be capable, Gomez somehow made his way to the top and his skills as a military commander are average at best." Castro observed.

"Gen. Gomez will be dealt with one way or the other as we both know. Worry about defeating the invaders and the rest shall follow in due time." Che advised.

"You are right of course comrade." Castro agreed.

"Political enemies are just as dangerous as the invaders. Gomez must be eliminated for the good of Cuba. He has failed to serve as a competent and most importantly lost your trust in his military capacity." Che commented.

"Gomez shall meet his proper end, relax we have a battle to focus on remember. You just smile and nod as if we have had a joke between us." Castro ordered.

SOUTH OF ORTIZ, CUBA,
5 MINUTES LATER:

ALVEREZ PEERED THROUGH HIS BINOCULARS AND SAW A LARGE FORMATION of Cuban soldiers heading into the jungle. He ordered the men to be ready for battle as a direct assault would soon be taking place. Capt. Vista knew that the brigade was close to being compelled to surrender, but for the time being they would fight on. Col. Alverez was not going to surrender until all of their ammo had been used up in combat. The Miami Brigade would continue to struggle for as long as possible as it was not a unit that gave up at the first sign of trouble.

Morale among the men in the brigade was still holding as they all shared a singular desire to survive and that propelled them to suppress most negative thoughts from coming to the surface. Alverez continued to rally spirits, but the reality of the situation was impossible to ignore or deny in any way. The members of the brigade knew that surrender was one of two possibilities with the other being a last stand. Feelings toward surrender were much stronger than fighting to the last man. The failure of the operation was enough; however no one wanted to die for a revolution that never truly got off the ground. Still until the order came from Alverez the men would fight as they had been trained, stoic and disciplined.

Cuban soldiers entered the jungle led by Gen. Gomez as they were under orders to engage with the invaders. Alverez had positioned his defensive line in a staggered formation to provide overlapping fire. The first Cuban scouts were quickly cut down before they could radio the exact positions of the invaders. Gomez ordered more of his men to search for weak points. Alverez heard that some of his men were running out of ammo. He ordered that bayonets be used and repeated that ammunition be taken off the bodies of the Cuban soldiers. AK-47s were a reliable weapon to use and the men eagerly turned to any source of firepower to combat the Cuban soldiers.

Gomez was still unable to punch through the invader's position and ordered his men to hold their position. More Cuban soldiers were required to drive back the members of the Miami Brigade. Before he was able to radio back to request reinforcements Gomez sustained a leg wound from one of the invaders. The bullet had struck the major artery in the right leg and blood was quickly flowing out of Gomez. Attempts to tie off the wound proved to be in vain as the general died less than a minute later from blood loss. The Miami Brigade continued to hold their position, but the need for ammo was reducing combat effectiveness as some of the men were out of bullets.

Alverez knew that more Cuban soldiers would soon be coming into the jungle.

In order to maximize the effectiveness of their limited ammo supply Alverez instructed his men redeploy in a shortened defensive line. The jungle would provide most of the cover and this was allowing the Miami Brigade to hold out against the larger Cuban forces. Causalities suffered by the brigade during the latest attack were a dozen killed and another dozen wounded. These were acceptable losses, but Alverez knew full well that if the brigade was forced back to the beach it would be wiped out by the Cuban Army. The decision to fight on was costing lives, but surrender would not be far off. Once most of the men were out of ammo the only option left for Alverez was to surrender.

ORTIZ, CUBA, 1 HOUR LATER:

CASTRO WAS GLAD TO BE RID OF GEN. GOMEZ, BUT SOMEONE WOULD be needed to replace him. Wanting an officer who could be trusted, Castro selected Gen. Cabas as during the struggle against Batista he had proven himself to be a brave and brilliant soldier time and again. Che agreed that Cabas was a good choice to replace Gomez as he too viewed the officer as one of the best in Cuba. Taking out a cigar Castro quickly summoned Cabas as he wanted to promote the officer on the spot. The colonel saluted and waited for Castro to address him. It did not take long for the Cuban leader to get right to the point:

"Col. Cabas, I need someone to replace Gomez and you have been selected for that role. I hereby promote you to the rank of general. You are to take two divisions and force the invaders back to Verde Beach. They are in that jungle and that must change before we can defeat them. I do not care how you accomplish this task, just get it done and compel those invaders to surrender. Killing them is not victory enough. I want to humiliate the USA and that means capturing the force they sent here. Do you have any questions about your assignment?" Castro asked.

"No sir, thank you sir." Cabas replied.

"Then get moving general as I expect positive results in two days or less." Castro ordered.

"Yes sir." Cabas confirmed.

Cabas saluted Castro and headed outside to take charge of the Cuban soldiers. He was tasked with driving back the invaders to Verde Beach at the Bay of Pigs. Castro had given the newly promoted general two days to carry out this assignment. With the clock officially ticking Cabas wasted no time in confronting the problem of how to force the invaders back. As the jungle was a difficult location to fight in Cabas came up with a simple plan. The general ordered his men to slowly converge on the invaders from two directions. It would take time for the plan to work, but with enough manpower Cabas could push back the invaders without having to fight them for every inch of jungle ground.

Castro spoke with Che after Cabas had left the room and discussed why the newly minted general was better than Gomez at being a commander:

"Cabas has a confidence in his style that Gomez lacked completely. Military commanders must be men who do not question themselves. Gomez was cautious and too afraid of his own shadow. Cabas is bold and does not worry about every little decision. The difference is all in character and it separates the great from the average as Gomez fell into the latter category." Castro explained.

"Yes I would agree with that assessment, but it goes far deeper as Gomez was trying to be something that he was not in the form of a competent general. Cabas can handle anything that is given to him. Gomez was always in need of help from other commanders." Che added.

"True, Gen. Gomez never showed himself to be a great military commander. Cabas on the other hand might be among the finest officers I have ever seen. Well in any case the matter of getting rid of Gomez has been taken care of by the invaders." Castro stated.

Castro was sure that Gen. Cabas could deal with the invaders and force them back where others had failed to produce results. The jungle would not be enough to stop the Cuban Army from completing its mission. Cabas was ready to launch his simple military tactic which had been used since the times of the Romans. Converging from two directions the Cubans were going to employ a simple pincer maneuver against the invaders. Cabas was curious was Gomez had insisted on using frontal assault tactics during his failed assault. This primitive tactic was ineffective against strong defensive lines.

APRIL 20, 1961,
VERDE BEACH, CUBA,
9:00 AM:

GEN. CABAS AND THE CUBAN ARMY HAD DRIVEN THE MEN OF THE Miami Brigade back to Verde Beach where the invasion had taken place some three days earlier. This forced a painful decision upon Col. Alverez as he could no longer the stark reality of the situation. Capt. Vista spoke with the colonel regarding the decision that had to be made about whether to surrender or not:

"We have come full circle as this is the same spot where the LSTs deposited us three days ago. Now I must raise the white flag and surrender the brigade. All of the blood and loss for nothing." Alverez stated.

"Sir we fought with all of our might and there is nothing shameful about surrender after such an effort. The men are out of ammo and food. Water is down to less than a three pints per man for one day. We have given all that could be asked of a unit under such dreadful conditions. The revolution failed, but we fought the Cuban Army for three long days. What more needs to be said about the courage of the Miami Brigade?" Vista asked.

"Nothing more needs to be said. I am the commander of the brigade and the time to surrender has finally arrived. While I detest running up the white flag it hopefully will spare the loss of the men. We have lost 114 good men and to continue fighting would doom the rest of us to their sad fate." Alverez observed.

"Sir surrender is the right course of action to take. We have given the full measure and then some. Our honor is satisfied. Hold your head high colonel." Vista added.

"You are right captain. Now if you will excuse me I have a white flag to wave.

Alverez tied a white shirt to a long stick and walked to the front of the brigade. All of the men began to lower their weapons as they hoped the Cuban Army would respect the white flag of surrender. Vista walked with Alverez and waved his arms to get the attention of some Cuban soldiers in the distance. A few seconds later a voice over a megaphone requested the commander of the invaders walk forward with his second in command. Alverez and Vista started towards the Cuban position with the white flag clutched tightly in the colonel's hand. Gen. Cabas waited for the opposing officers to reach his position before greeting them. The conversation went along the lines of an official surrender:

"I am Col. Alverez and I command the Miami Brigade. I am here to officially surrender the entire brigade to the Cuban Army. All of our supplies are depleted and further resistance is impossible." Alverez admitted.

"My name is Gen. Cabas and I accept your surrender on behalf of the Cuban Army. You are to order your men to place their weapons on the ground and slow walk to our location with their hands up. If you try any tricks all of the men will be shot. Do you understand my commands at how the brigade will surrender?" Cabas inquired.

"Yes I do." Alverez stated.

"Good, then you may proceed with the surrender and return here once that task has been completed. Your men fought well, but whatever you were trying with that invasion several days ago has failed." Cabas added.

Alverez offered a salute to Cabas and returned to the brigade with Vista to command the men to lay down their weapons and officially surrender. It was an order that the colonel had dreaded since things started to go wrong with the invasion. There was silence as Cabas ordered to be quiet for the next few minutes. The general wanted to enjoy the moment in peace without the noise created by the Cuban soldiers. Cabas ordered Castro be informed of the surrender of the invaders at once. The failed invasion had resulted in nothing other than a three day exercise in futility.

Alverez and Vista returned to the Miami Brigade as the order to lay down their weapons was given. Wanting to end the sad military affair all of the men compiled with the order without question. Each of the men displayed either a stoic face or a tired one. Mentally the members of the Miami Brigade were ready to surrender as they had been pushed back to the very location where all of their hardships began in Cuba. Weary from their long ordeal the men of the Miami Brigade formed up and made their way to the Cuban Army position. Alverez led the brigade and he kept his held up as Vista was right about there being nothing more to prove.

Cabas ordered pictures be taken of the surrender and cameras began snapping away to capture the entire scene for the Cuban Army and the world. All of the weapons of the Miami Brigade were collected and sorted by type with six piles of rifles, machineguns, carbines, pistols, bayonets and bazookas being created. While the LSTs were gone the wreckage of the freighter could easily be photographed as it was only 300 yards from the beach. Cabas looked at the men of the Miami Brigade and then ordered that pictures of Verde Beach be taken for use as a propaganda tool.

With the surrender of the Miami Brigade the men were driven off to the prisons in Havana in cargo trucks which had been used to deliver supplies to the Cuban Army. Castro had not yet made up his mind on the fate of the invaders. He wanted to make an example of the Miami Brigade, but this could wait as he wished to enjoy the fruits of the victory that had just been achieved. Cabas knew this his career was going to improve thanks to the victory over the invaders. Celebrations broke out among the Cuban soldiers as they had prevailed against a force that was intent on their destruction. Cabas was content to take pictures of the Bay of Pigs and all that had taken place there. He believed that an important moment in the history of Cuba had just taken place.

PRESIDENT KENNEDY WAS LIVID WITH THE CIA AS THE ENTIRE PLAN to overthrow Castro had gone awry starting with the invasion four days earlier. The Kennedy Administration had egg all over its face from the entire debacle. Agent Malone was called in to answer for the sins of the CIA with Kennedy letting loose his rage at the total failure of Operation Zapata to achieve any of its goals. Malone did his best to remain calm despite the verbal assault that he endured from Kennedy. It was a one sided conversation for the most part with Malone staying quiet and letting the president vent his displeasure with the outcome of Operation Zapata:

"Castro is still in power and the Miami Brigade has been compelled to surrender! Now the survivors are prisoners whose fate might be death thanks to woeful failures of the CIA in the planning and execution of this debacle that was Operation Zapata! What do you have to say for yourself or the CIA that can explain this poor showing by the Miami Brigade?" Kennedy inquired.

"Mr. President with all due respect not all operations turn out as expected. This was an example of where the plans were unable to be turned into reality. The loss of the Miami Brigade is unfortunate, but the revolution failed to take place as clearly Castro's grip on the people of Cuba was stronger than we expected. Operations like this are gambles no matter how many precautions are taken by the planners." Malone admitted.

"The failure still stings and makes my administration look incompetent in foreign policy. We are engaged in a battle of reputation with the Soviet Union. Our failures are their successes. Premier Khrushchev is on top of the world right now as Castro is a close ally of his. Now we have failed publicly to remove the Cuban leader and the fallout has just begun." Kennedy explained.

Malone had made a point that all operations were a gamble, but Kennedy still felt sore that the CIA failed to execute a plan that promised to remove Castro. There was no silver lining to the entire episode as now some 1,286 surviving members of the Miami Brigade were prisoners in Cuba. Kennedy vowed never to trust the CIA again with such a massive military project as that job needed to be handled by the Pentagon. Malone was excused from the Oval Office as Kennedy had vented enough for one day. The CIA had promised too much and delivered too little with Operation Zapata. Partly Kennedy blamed himself for trusting the CIA instead of asking the hard questions.

The Bay of Pigs Invasion had been a painful reminder of what could go wrong with a military operation. Two goals to start a revolution and remove Castro were both so straightforward that Kennedy believed they could be achieved by Operation Zapata. Eisenhower and Truman encouraged Kennedy to green light the invasion. In the end nothing went right with Operation Zapata as each component seemed to fall apart. The air power did not deal with the entire Cuban Air Force and no revolution took place upon the invasion. Kennedy would take full responsibility for the failure of Operation Zapata.

Despite the blunders by the CIA, Kennedy would not attempt to claim that he had nothing to do with the entire effort to remove Castro. He promised himself and his cabinet that in the future things would be different, but for the moment he had to face the nation. Americans were aware of only the basic details of Operation Zapata. News reports mostly came from information obtained by the Cuban Army as they took enough pictures and video to create a documentary. Kennedy would appear on the national news and place himself as the man who ordered Operation Zapata.

APRIL 26, 1961,
MOSCOW, RUSSIA,
1:30 PM:

PREMIER KHRUSHCHEV WAS AMAZED BY HOW INCOMPETENT THE United States could be. President Kennedy had taken responsibility for the failure of Operation Zapata. It was a move which Khrushchev saw as a sign of weakness as in the Soviet Union the government never showed itself to the people as anything other than a strong ruler that controlled all parts of their lives. By admitting mistakes were made Kennedy showed himself to be a leader that was accountable. Khrushchev had called Castro shortly after Kennedy made his speech to congratulate him on repulsing the poor American effort to unseat the Cuban leader from power.

In reality not only had Castro thwarted the US effort to remove him, but the Soviet Union could continue to use Cuban as a staging ground. It was a positive situation for both the Communist nations. Khrushchev saw Kennedy as weak and too green to lead America. This perception was reinforced by the failed Bay of Pigs Invasion in which the US showed itself to be incapable of properly taking out an unfriendly nation some 90 miles from its very shores. Khrushchev was thinking ahead for what Cuba could be used for and the idea of placing nuclear missiles entered into his mind. While the timing was not yet right, Khrushchev saw a desperate need to counter American nuclear missiles in Turkey.

While the Soviet Union was a powerful military force in the world it wanted to gain an advantage over the US and placing nuclear missiles in Cuba would tip the scales in favor of Russia. Khrushchev wanted to place Russia in a position where it could dictate terms to the US instead of having to contend with a first strike policy. He saw Cuba as the perfect base to setup nuclear missiles at as it was a fellow Communist nation that had just prevailed over the United States. Khrushchev wrote down his inner thoughts on the subject for later reference:

"Castro has survived an attempt to remove him from power by the United States. This means that Cuba will not fall prey to the tendency by America to replace any government in the Western Hemisphere it does not approve of as it did in the 1920s. Castro has shown himself to be a capable leader and the Soviet Union can use this fact to its own advantage. Currently there are nuclear missiles in Turkey which give the US a first strike capacity. If Russian nuclear missiles were to be placed in Cuba it would give the Soviet Union an ability to have a first strike capacity of its own. Russia must be kept strong as weakness is rewarded with total disaster as was the case in the Great Patriotic War in the early stages where the German Army raced towards Moscow and got within 40 miles of reaching the city. Stalin had trusted Hitler in 1939 when a nonaggression treaty was signed and in 1941 that trust nearly cost Russia the war and its very existence. I must show the United States that strength can work both ways. Turkey is a staging ground for America and Cuba will be a powerful staging ground for Russia." Khrushchev wrote.

The exact timing for the placement of nuclear missiles into Cuba would wait until 1962. Khrushchev wanted to focus his attention on the Soviet Space Program which was proving itself to a propaganda coup. In addition the situation in Cuba needed to cool down as Khrushchev believed that all precautions needed to be taken before nuclear missiles were sent to be setup only 90 miles from the shores of the United States. The key was for secrecy to take place until all the nuclear missiles were already setup in Cuba. Khrushchev would not be informing any members of the Politburo of the drastic action. He did not have to answer to anyone in Russia. It was a bold move by Khrushchev as the consequences of failure might lead to nuclear war.

From Khrushchev's point of view the Soviet Union was threatened by the US nuclear missiles in Turkey and this gave them the right to place their own missiles into Cuba as a way of balancing the situation. Kennedy was seen as weak and Khrushchev was daring enough to try and push around the American leader. All of this would wait until fall of 1962 as Khrushchev felt no urgency to rush such an ambitious project. He believed that Cuba could serve the needs of the Soviet Union and bring the two nations closer together. Castro had a good working relationship with Khrushchev which could be used if the plan to place nuclear missiles in Cuba came to pass.

PRISONERS OF WAR

CHAPTER 9

APRIL 30, 1961,
HAVANA, CUBA,
8:30 AM:

A PAIR OF HEAVILY ARMED CUBAN GUARDS STOOD OUTSIDE THE CELL where Alverez and Vista were both being held. A finely dressed man appeared outside the cell with a smile on his face. He carried a piece of paper and pen and was dressed in a fine suit. As the senior officers of the brigade Alverez and Vista were kept away from the other prisoners. The Cuban in the suit spoke in a clear voice to state his reason for coming to the prison:

"My name is Rico Estevez and I work for Castro with his political issues. I have here a piece of paper that states the Miami Brigade was funded and trained in the United States to come here to Cuba and attempt an overthrow of Castro and his government. There are two signature lines at the bottom. You will both sign this piece of paper or the surviving members of the brigade shall be shot as a result. Castro wants to have written confirmation that the United States was involved and as both of you were senior officers your signatures will be enough to satisfy his suspicions." Estevez explained.

"I want your solemn word that the men of the brigade shall not be harmed once that paper is signed by us. We must have confirmation ourselves." Alverez demanded.

"Col. Alverez you may have my word and the word of Castro himself that once that paper is signed the men of the brigade are safe from harm." Estevez assured.

"Then we shall sign the paper." Alverez confirmed.

"I am glad to see that you believe in saving the lives of the men under your command." Estevez added.

While Alverez detested having to sign any document that admitted fault, he could not ignore the reality of the situation was not in his favor. If Castro wanted to all of the men of the Miami Brigade could be shot. Preventing this outcome was foremost on the colonel's mind. Vista came to a similar conclusion as he quickly placed his signature beneath that of Alverez. Having both signed the paper Estevez smiled and left the room as quickly as he had entered it. Alverez highly doubted that Castro would spare the entire brigade, but if even some of the members were saved because of signing the statement it would be worth it.

Finally having made up his mind about what to do with the prisoners, Castro would let most of them live to serve as a reminder of failure to the United States. However a few would be put on a trial and then executed for trying to bring down the Cuban Government. Alverez and Vista were safe from these trials as they were the leaders of the Miami Brigade. Castro wanted to eliminate officers that were not among the senior staff of the unit. He wished to show the United States and the Soviet Union that no one would challenge his power in Cuba. Officially the US had not said a word about the Miami Brigade, but there were unofficial channels being used to learn about the possibility of releasing the men.

Kennedy could not afford to wash his hands of the Miami Brigade. This was a large group of men that were prisoners in Cuba instead of a single spy or small team. For the moment Castro held all of the cards when it came to the fate of the Miami Brigade. Asking for the release of the men would not amount to anything until the US gained leverage over Castro. It did not appear that this would happen and Kennedy could do nothing other than wait for an opportunity to obtain the release of the members of the Miami Brigade.

Conditions for the surviving members of the brigade were barely tolerable. The prison itself had dated from the days of Batista and Castro left much of the structure as it was upon coming to power. Trials and executions were held in the nearby courtyard. A firing squad would be used to kill anyone found guilty in the trials. Justice was swift under Castro and the trials were merely a way of appearing legal. In reality anyone who angered the Cuban leader would find themselves imprisoned for life on trumped up charges or executed. These were the only outcomes as no one served for five years or got parole for good behavior.

THE WHITE HOUSE, 2 DAYS LATER:

PRESIDENT KENNEDY RECEIVED A BRIEFING ON THE STATUS OF THE men of the Miami Brigade. All of the prisoners were in Havana and their future was not good from any point of view. Even if Castro spared their lives it would be to spend the rest of their days in prison. Malone had been called in to speculate on the actions of Castro as there was no reliable intelligence on his next move. Malone did his best to predict the future:

"Castro has the political clout to do as he wishes and the failure of the Bay of Pigs Invasion also has weakened the United States in the eyes of the Soviet Union. The lives of the Miami Brigade prisoners are in peril and there is nothing that can be done to change that fact. We can try and bargain for the release of the men, but the price is not going to be cheap. Castro has this administration over a barrel at the moment. If he decides to ask for a high price for the men then we would be forced to either pay and lose face or refuse and lose even more face. The American people are probably shaking their collective heads in total disbelief of the current situation. Castro might hold a few trials and the outcome will be death sentences for the men taking part in them. This is a black eye for the United States." Malone predicted.

"Thank you for your candid assessment, getting those men back alive is important to me. They all risked their lives and the least that can be done is bring back those we sent into harm's way. We sold them a fantasy of a revolution which failed to take place. Now the only goal is seeing how many make it back to these shores. Castro can take whatever action he chooses, however I think that he will spare most of the Miami Brigade survivors. He wants the court of public opinion to see him as a great leader. Killing some 1,286 men would forever paint Castro as a butcher. Still I fear that some of the men are going to be executed." Kennedy remarked.

Obtaining the freedom of the Miami Brigade would require patience as the United States was not in a strong position to dictate terms. Castro could afford to wait for months or even years before sending his official reply.

Che and Raul both wanted the prisoners to be executed; however Castro saw the value in keeping most of them alive to please public opinion. Kennedy wanted to bring back the men for two reasons. First the brigade had put their lives on the line. Second the White House could use any form of positive public relations. Bringing back an entire brigade of men from the clutches of Cuba would do wonders to paint Kennedy as a capable leader.

Malone knew the CIA was still in the doghouse as it had grossly misled Kennedy on how easy the operation to remove Castro would be. Even so there was a need to oppose the Soviet Union by whatever means required and the CIA was an important part of this opposition. Malone did his best to prove to Kennedy that not all the agents at the CIA were trying to sugarcoat things. This impression was hard to shake following the failure of the Bay of Pigs Invasion. Trust between Kennedy and the CIA would have to be built on a shared desire to oppose the Soviet Union. Anything more than this common goal would be asking too much of Kennedy or the CIA. What to do about the Miami Brigade prisoners was a question that required an answer.

Both McNamara and Robert Kennedy detested the CIA leaders and wanted to sack several of them. This action would only expose the fact that the United States had an agency that was failing. President Kennedy felt that there was plenty of blame for the Bay of Pigs Invasion ending as it did. Getting the Miami Brigade survivors back was more important to Kennedy that firing CIA officials. Castro was still in power and removing him seemed an impossible goal at this point short of a US invasion of Cuba which Kennedy ruled out. This was a time to be patient instead of endorsing rash actions. Malone had proven to Kennedy that some of the senior agents in the CIA could be trusted.

MAY 10, 1961,
HAVANA, CUBA,
10:30 AM:

COL. ALVEREZ AND CAPT. VISTA HEARD SEVERAL GUNSHOTS RING OUT less than 200 feet away from their prison cell. Ten officers of the Miami Brigade had been found guilty of attempting to start a revolution against Castro. All of the trials were for show only with no attempt to give the defendants any form of defense. This was a message to both the surviving members of the Miami Brigade and the United States that Castro had complete control over the fate of the men. Alverez spoke with Vista shortly after the executions were carried out:

"It would have been better for those poor officers to die in combat than shot like cattle after show trials. It is a terrible way to meet one's end." Alverez commented.

"True, but they went to their deaths like men as not one of them cried or attempted to beg for mercy. They served the Miami Brigade and paid the ultimate price for that service to the unit. I share your feelings, but Castro has total control over our fate. We might join have our lives cut short by that dictator. Whatever lies in store for us the Miami Brigade was our greatest achievement. I think that Maj. Rodriquez would have agreed with me if he were here. Those officers knew the risks and they fought for what they believed in." Vista added.

"That they did, but now they are dead by the hands of a firing squad instead meeting their end like soldiers. It is a pity we did not have more supplies as I would have liked to fight to bloody last stand. Instead our lack of ammo compelled me to surrender. Now we are in limbo awaiting our fate." Alverez reflected.

"At times like these we must have faith that God is watching our plight. More importantly we must have faith that a solution can be found to our problems as there is nothing else that will solve our situation other than faith and hope." Vista insisted.

The execution of the ten officers hit Alverez hard as he felt fully responsible for the brigade members becoming prisoners. Vista viewed the executions as being Castro's cruel action and not the fault of the colonel. As prisoners the men were forced to listen to a speech each day from the propaganda minister. These speeches were created to help instill socialism into all men and women in Cuba. Alverez and Vista did not really mind the speeches as they broke up an otherwise boring routine. Exercise was permitted for 30 minutes each day for the men. This one activity helped lift the spirits of the brigade members.

Fear of being tortured or executed was a constant companion for the prisoners and they coped in many different ways. Some attempted to ignore the fear by keeping busy in any way they could. Others embraced a more fatalistic viewpoint. Alverez and Vista did their best to encourage the other men by writing letters which were passed during exercise time. These letters were filled with jokes and stories that each contained happy outcomes or funny endings. Vista did most of the writing while Alverez added in his own sentiments.

Vista composed a new letter to the men as he felt that the execution of the 10 officers deserved some form of response by the captain and colonel:

"During these dark times we must all have hope that our fate shall be vastly different from the brave men killed by Castro's soldiers. They served the Miami Brigade as brave officers and shall be remembered by all of us for their stoic departure from this world. Our hearts and minds are filled with sadness, yet we must have both faith and hope. We shall strive to outlive this prison and this terrible moment in our journey through life. We are the members of the Miami Brigade and our fate is not written in stone, but hinges upon luck and perhaps even providence itself." Vista wrote.

Alverez carefully read over the letter and added in a few sentences to inspire the men. He wanted to send a message that they were still a community instead of merely prisoners located together. Other men in the prison were there for political reasons as true criminals took up less than 50% of the cells. Crime in Cuba was relatively low while political oppression could be found on every street corner. The members of Miami Brigade were among the thousands that were enemies of Castro. For many of these political prisoners their disappearance confirmed they had been killed. Records of prisoners were rudimentary, while the execution lists were kept in meticulous order.

JUNE 21, 1961,
THE WHITE HOUSE,
10:45 AM:

WANTING TO SHOW THAT THE UNITED STATES WAS SERIOUS ABOUT obtaining the release of the Miami Brigade the president assigned Robert Kennedy to the task of secret talks with the Cuban leadership. It was a move which surprised the attorney general. He demanded to know why someone else could not be given this difficult task.

President Kennedy was direct in why his brother was selected for this assignment:

"Castro believes we are not ready to seriously bargain for the release of the Miami Brigade. He knows that we need to keep up appearances. As a senior member of my cabinet you are the perfect man to complete this task. If the Cuban officials hear that Robert Kennedy is going to negotiate the release the Miami Brigade I promise you all of them will take notice. Castro himself will look upon the talks as more serious than before. Now do you want to argue the point further?" Kennedy asked.

"No, I will begin the secret talks. I disagreed with the Bay of Pigs Invasion and it is fitting that I will play a part in bringing those men home." Robert replied.

"Good I am glad to see that you have changed your opinion of these secret talks. Now remember I want those men back in the quickest way possible. These secret talks are the best way of keeping the media away from the issue." Kennedy stated.

"What do you think our chances are of getting back the survivors at this point?" Robert inquired.

"Not promising at this time." Kennedy answered.

Robert Kennedy would begin the secret talks with Estevez in Cuba. If the media somehow got word of the negotiations the entire affair would be terminated at once under the guise of plausible deniability. For the moment President Kennedy did not expect any results, but sooner or later the United States Government would be able to improve its bargaining position with Cuba. Obtaining the release of the Miami Brigade survivors was a necessary step to save face for the Kennedy Administration. If the talks could produce positive results before the end of the first term President Kennedy could claim victory.

Media coverage of the failed Bay of Pigs Invasion was continuing to draw attention from the American public. This made any topic that had a connection with the failed revolution a headline. Any form of talks with Cuba was obviously something that the Kennedy Administration wanted to keep a secret. Once a bargain was reached for the Miami Brigade to be returned to the United States then the veil of secrecy would be lifted. This process was expected to take several months at least. Castro did not want to part with the Miami Brigade until he received something of equal value in return. He sought to gain financial compensation for the release of the men.

JULY 17, 1961,
HAVANA, CUBA,
8:30 AM:

ALL OF THE SURVIVING MEMBERS OF THE MIAMI BRIGADE EXCEPT Alverez and Vista were brought to a large room that was used for prisoner exercise. Castro walked over to a podium to deliver an important announcement. He was escorted by a dozen soldiers armed with AK-47s. Raul and Che were present as well standing just behind and to the left of Castro. There was a brief moment of silence before the Cuban leader addressed all of the men gathered in front of him. Then Castro spoke using his arms to punctuate his passionate mood. Alverez and Vista were kept from the address to prevent their presence from influencing the men. Castro wanted his message to get through and by keeping Both Alverez and Vista in their cell this was possible. Speaking in a candid manner Castro looked directly at the men:

"It has been three months since your failed revolution took place at the Bay of Pigs. During that time you have been kept alive to humiliate the United States. Some of your officers have been executed and your stay at this prison has been a most unpleasant one. This is all due to the United States failing to support the invasion with all it had to offer. The US Government abandoned you to fend for yourselves on those beaches. Now I will give you a chance to leave this awful place behind and all of the sufferings it has caused. I have with me a piece of paper which states that the Bay of Pigs Invasion was a terrible plot of the United States. In addition this paper says that you renounce your part in the invasion and turn your back on the United States. Those of you that sign this piece of paper shall be released at once. You will be free from prison and given a small amount of money to start your life again in Cuba." Castro explained.

None of the surviving members of the Miami Brigade moved towards Castro to sign the paper. Knowing the consequences of signing the document the men sat where they were without hesitation. They had each taken part in the invasion out of their own free will. To renounce that failed action would be to be turning their back on their own principles. As the seconds past by it became clear that no one would be stepping forward to renounce the Bay of Pigs Invasion. Castro allowed several minutes to pass before ordering the men returned to their cells. Che spoke with the Cuban leader after the prisoners had left the room:

"It would appear that their stubbornness is stronger than either of us expected." Che observed.

"Those men are fools and perhaps even brave fools at that

as they volunteer to return to prisoner. They want to remember the Bay of Pigs Invasion as a glorious defeat instead of a pointless tragedy. The United States sent these brave fools to start a revolution and gave them a meager force to do so with." Castro commented.

"They fought with courage for a cause that each of them believed in. Is that not what all rebels do? Were we any different a few years ago?" Che asked.

"Comrade we fought in the jungle yes, but we fought with enough support to sustain our guerrilla war. These misguided fools fought with the equivalent of sticks and stones against a mighty elephant. Now to kill an elephant with sticks and stones requires superior manpower until the beast is brought down." Castro added.

"Perhaps in a few more months some will sign that piece of paper. Time has a way of weakening the soul and that goes doubly true for prison." Che predicted.

"Indeed, but I have feeling these brave fools are going to be stubborn to the very end. There is no point in killing them as it would not change any of their minds. Making martyrs is not in our best interests." Castro pointed out.

"At least the United States and President Kennedy have been taught a painful lesson on how not to invade a nation of passionate people." Che remarked.

"When these prisoners are returned the United States will pay a high price to obtain that freedom for the brave fools they sent on a mission of folly. That is a lesson I hope the US never forgets. Cuba is not a nation that can be invaded by a bunch of amateurs that." Castro stressed.

Both Castro and Che viewed the prisoners as a pawn that could be used to obtain something of great value from the United States. Until a bargain could be struck the Miami Brigade survivors were to remain prisoners for their crimes. Alverez and Vista suspected that the recent address by Castro was some kind of a deal to get the men to renounce the invasion. Several letters had been read to the Miami Brigade members that stated why the Bay of Pigs Invasion was justified. In addition the assistance of the United States was lauded as being one of the most generous backings that any unit had ever received by another nation. While Alverez and Vista had stretched the truth on the last part they managed to get their point across.

Prepared for the argument that Castro might use the men of the Miami Brigade were able to resist the urge to blame the United States or their own leaders. There was also the fact that Alverez and Vista were trusted by the men as leaders of the Miami Brigade. Castro was asking too much of the men to turn their backs on the invasion and the United States. It had been a move which showed how much both sides did not understand the other. All of the prisoners were loyal to their leaders and to the US for providing the military assistance. Castro believed that his personality could win over anyone. This proved to be wrong as the prisoners did not sign the paper that would have granted their freedom.

AUGUST 12, 1961,
THE WHITE HOUSE,
1:30 PM:

ROBERT KENNEDY BEGAN ANOTHER SECRET TALK WITH ESTEVEZ regarding the release of the Miami Brigade. As with the four previous conversations between the men there was little common ground that both sides could agree upon. Estevez was under strict orders from Castro to ask for a large sum of money from the United States in the area of 100 million dollars. This figure was too much for either President Kennedy or the American people to accept. Castro knew that his terms were out of the ballpark and did this wanting the United States to refuse the deal. Robert Kennedy pressed forward with the talks doing all he could to lower the price demanded by Estevez.

This back and forth between Estevez and Robert was proving futile as the two sides were no closer to a deal than at the beginning of the talks several months earlier. Still the Kennedy Administration was relentless in its pursuit of the release of the Miami Brigade prisoners. President Kennedy wanted to show the American public that he would not abandon the prisoners. With all of the failures of the Bay of Pigs Invasion the president did not wish to add any more to its aftermath. Robert Kennedy did his best to appear flexible in the talks, but Estevez could not move from his hardline position insisted upon by Castro under fear of death:

"Cuba must be paid a high price in compensation for its return of the Miami Brigade. We are within our right to demand this large sum of 100 million dollars. It was the men of this force that invaded our nation. Castro wanted to execute all of the survivors, but received advice not to make martyrs out of the men. They are in prison and the men shall remain there until the United States sees fit to give in to our reasonable terms. Castro is a leader who knows the value of a good deal. Cuba deserves a good deal after enduring an invasion from these traitors. If I were you I would persuade your brother to accept this offer while it still is on the table." Estevez explained.

"The United States does not accept offers that are out of the ballpark and these terms fit that description. You are asking for a sum that is far too high. These terms must be lowered before any deal is struck." Robert countered.

"As I have stated many times before this deal is based upon what Castro demands. I have no power to adjust the terms of the deal. I am required to answer for my actions in the same way that you are forced to justify yours to our superiors." Estevez insisted.

"Then these talks will have to continue at a later time as right now I am needed elsewhere." Robert added.

"I look forward to our next conversation as we are both getting very good at convincing the other that the terms of the deal are not favorable to our respective nations and their leaders." Estevez joked.

In reality Robert Kennedy did not need to leave, but he felt the conversation was proving futile. With no set time for the deal to be struck the two parties could afford to go in circles for the moment. Castro and Kennedy were not in the mood to compromise as they both believed their side was justified in digging in its heels. The fate of the prisoners was more a question of time than anything else as they were a pawn in the greater political chess match between the United States and Cuba. The talks would continue, but Robert Kennedy understood that he was talking instead of making progress. A lower price would have to be agreed up before a deal was made.

ALVEREZ AND VISTA HAD BOTH COMPOSED A NEW LETTER TO BE SENT out to the men of the brigade. With the exercise period about to take place it would soon be time to send the letter on its short journey several rooms over. So far the guards had failed to notice the delivery of the letters as they were more content to watch for anyone who tried to escape or cause trouble. Alverez wanted to keep the morale of men up during these trying times. If the letters could be read on a weekly basis it would serve as a way of transmitting hope to the men of the brigade. Rotting away in prison took a toll on the human spirit. Both of the officers were aware that temptation to renounce the revolution and United States existed.

Keeping the morale of the men up on a daily basis was just as important as food and water. Alverez and Vista each took a letter with them to double the chances that their message would get through. Armed guards escorted the officers to the exercise area and kept watch over all of the men as ordered. Alverez signaled Vista to distract the guards in some form while he delivered the letter to one of the brigade members. Vista was aware that his performance had to be convincing. He pretended to faint and this drew the immediate attention of the guards. Seconds later Alverez passed the letter without being noticed to a member of the brigade. Vista's distraction had proven effective as he gained the full attention of all the guards in the exercise yard temporarily.

Alverez gave the signal for Vista to end his distraction and soon the captain was back on his feet. None of the guards had gotten close as they did not care if one of the officers perished for any reason. Castro gave orders for the guards to act only if the prisoners were causing a disturbance. Vista spoke with Alverez less than a minute after the letter was delivered:

"We are taking risks with these letter delivers that might make the situation worse for the men if anything goes wrong during the transfer." Vista commented.

"It is a risk that must be taken for the sake of morale of the brigade. These men survive on more than food and water as their spirits must be kept alive as well. Letters written by their senior officers are all we can do to keep morale up. Isolated from the brigade except for this brief exercise time letters are all we have to offer. Risk is part of all endeavors in life." Alverez stressed.

"Caution must be taken and I suppose that if we keep up the distractions these transfers can go on for months before they are detected. Still sooner or later our luck will probably run out." Vista predicted.

"Until then we send the messages." Alverez confirmed.

Alverez was not ignorant of the dangers of passing letters within eyesight of the guards. However there was no other option as the senior officers were isolated from the rest of the prisoners. Risks had to be taken in some form or another for the letters to exchange hands. This method could continue until it was discovered which Alverez hoped would not be for several months. Already the transfers had gone on for over 120 days. Vista had come up with several forms of distraction that seemed to work quite effectively. His fainting performance was the most dramatic; however there were others that required all of the focus of the captain. Alverez could still serve as a leader even behind bars of an enemy nation.

CHAPTER 10

A BITTER TRADE

NOVEMBER 29, 1962,
THE WHITE HOUSE,
9:30 AM:

THE RECENT CUBAN MISSILE CRISIS HAD BROUGHT THE ENTIRE WORLD to the brink of World War III. It also had given the United States political leverage to demand the release of the Miami Brigade. President Kennedy showed Cuba and the Soviet Union that he was a powerful leader as Khrushchev had been forced to back down and promise to remove the nuclear missiles from Cuba. Now was the perfect time for Robert Kennedy to press the issue of obtaining the release of the Miami Brigade. Castro was irate that the Soviet Union had refused to be aggressive and run the blockade the United States imposed on Cuba.

Castro was disappointed with Khrushchev and wanted nothing more to do with the Miami Brigade. All of the survivors were a constant reminder of Castro's conflict with the United States. Wishing to get rid of the men as quickly as possible, Castro instructed Estevez to reach an agreement with Robert Kennedy. A large sum of money would be traded for the release of the Miami Brigade. It was the least that Castro could accept as a fair deal. The amount of money demanded by Cuba had dropped from 100 million to 43 million dollars in farm equipment. This reduction was enough to allow for progress in the talks between Robert Kennedy and Estevez.

Leverage over Cuba had finally been obtained by the United States as Castro was embarrassed by the fallout from the Cuban Missile Crisis. Robert Kennedy knew that the terms were not going to improve over 43 million and suggested to his brother that the deal be accepted. The surviving members of the Miami Brigade would be released in late-December if the terms of the agreement were accepted. President Kennedy discussed the matter with Robert to make sure nothing was being overlooked:

"Castro has held the advantage ever since the failure of the Bay of Pigs Invasion. It is extremely nice to have the upper hand for a change." Kennedy stated.

"How true, now all we have to do is accept the terms of the deal and the survivors of the Miami Brigade will be returned to the United States in exactly one month from now after being held for over a year." Robert added.

"The sum of 43 million dollars in farm equipment is a bitter trade to make, but it has to be done to obtain the freedom of the Miami Brigade." Kennedy observed.

"Agreed, Castro is still receiving a king's ransom for the release of the Miami Brigade. He has something that this administration wants in the form of those survivors. All these months of secret talks finally are going to pay off as those men are coming home. They deserve a hero's welcome for each of them placed life and limb on the line trying to overthrow Castro. The failure of the operation was unfortunate, but getting those men back is the last piece of unfinished business with Cuba. I for one am glad to be ending my phone calls with Estevez. He is a man that spent countless hours wasting my time until most recently." Robert explained.

"I thank you for your efforts as this deal would not have been reached without your patience and persistence in talking with Estevez. Perhaps Castro simply grew tired of holding the prisoners." Kennedy commented.

"More likely he has no further use for them. We have been

humiliated for over a year with the aftermath of the Bay of Pigs Invasion." Robert suggested.

With a date promised for the return of the men all that was required was for President Kennedy to agree to the terms of the deal. Although paying off Castro was not a pleasant action it would gain the end result of getting the prisoners back. Kennedy instructed his brother to accept the terms of the bargain the next day. Paying Cuba off in farm equipment was the necessary price for the return of the Miami Brigade. While this was the Cold War some deals could be made between Capitalist and Communist nations. Kennedy despised Castro, but for the present nothing could be done to eliminate him.

NOVEMBER 30, 1962, HAVANA, CUBA, 1:30 PM:

CASTRO ORDERED ALL THE MEN OF THE MIAMI BRIGADE TO BE brought to the exercise yard. He was going to deliver the news himself. Che and Raul were not present this time as the Cuban leader did not want them to be there. Castro was glad that a deal with the United States had finally been reached. The prisoners were of no real value and in exchange for their freedom tons of farm equipment was going to be sent to Cuba. Both nations would gain from the arrangement with Castro getting the better side of the bargain. Kennedy would finally bring all loose ends of the Bay of Pigs Invasion to a close. Castro mentioned a deal with the United States had been reached:

"President Kennedy has finally decided that a deal for your release should be agreed to. All of you are going back to the United States in late-December. Cuba is gaining from this deal as well and therefore you have served your purpose as a bargaining chip. Cuba will be glad that you are leaving. Trying to start a revolution is a crime that few in this country are excused from. You are all lucky to be alive. I detest what you attempt to do and your bravery was in pursuit of a failed operation. I wish to rid myself of you all and that is why this deal shall be honored at this time." Castro announced.

Speaking with total candor Castro had made his point clear to the brigade that they were merely a bargaining chip in politics. The Cuban leader loathed their actions and was acting to gain monetary goods for the nation. None of the men in the brigade cared about the reasons for their return to the United States. They were simply glad to be leaving the prison in just under one month. Alverez and Vista smiled as their efforts to keep the morale of the men up had prevailed. With the exception of the 10 officers who were executed the surviving men of the brigade would be leaving prison on their own two feet just as they had entered it.

After Castro spoke the men were allowed to enjoy their exercise time which gave Alverez a chance to address the members of the Miami Brigade directly. He wasted no time as sending letters never had the same impact as speaking direct to the men:

"We are going back to the United States and that shall be our permanent home. This brigade made an attempt to return to Cuba and remove Castro. That effort failed and we must all accept this fact. Freedom can be found some 90 miles north of here in the United States. There are tens of thousands of Cubans in Miami and that is our culture. Cuba is the land of our birth, however freedom is more important than the dirt upon we stand. Freedom is worth dying for and land is merely a place on the map. Cuba will always have a tender place in our hearts, but we must live in reality not emotions." Alverez explained.

While the men did not cheer as it would have attracted the attention of the guards they were glad to see their commander in person. Reading letters for months was just not the same as a physical presence. Hearing the news that a deal had been reached for their freedom also boosted their morale to a new high. Not since the start of the invasion had the men of the Miami Brigade felt so eager about an upcoming event. A light at the end of the tunnel could now be seen by all the prisoners. Castro left the prison glad to be getting rid of the Miami Brigade in a manner that benefitted Cuba.

GUARDS CALLED FOR THE END OF THE EXERCISE PERIOD WHICH MEANT it was time for the prisoners to be returned to their cells at once. Alverez and Vista could finally plan for something more exciting than writing the next letter to the men. Countdown calendars were created by both the officers and men of the Miami Brigade. Freedom was coming in less than a month to all of them. Months of not knowing their fate were over for the brigade. Castro had delivered the best piece of news the men could have asked for in prison. Prison life would not damper the spirits of the Miami Brigade. They had an endgame to their unpleasant time in Havana. Survival was now a matter of counting off the days until freedom.

Alverez and Vista wrote one final letter to the men to ask that they remember their actions as being ones that were necessary to the cause of freedom:

"We have taken part in history and though that effort failed it must not be forgotten or downplayed. Cuba is our nation of origin. While we may strong disagree with its leaders the people are not our enemies. They serve the current leader because they have no choice. Castro is a man that leads by fear not by respect. Our stay in Cuba has taught us that all the citizens of this nation are his prisoners not just the Miami Brigade. They are prisoners of the mind as much as the body. I will be glad to be returning to the United States. There are many freedoms in that nation that are absent from Cuba. I worked for Batista and his vices were many, but they never sucked the life out of Cuba as Castro has." Alverez wrote.

Vista and Alverez were overjoyed that their prison time would soon be ending. Being separated from the men except for exercise time was a hardship which tried the souls of the senior officers. Writing the letters had kept their morale up as well as their sanity. Both men were under more stress than the rest of the brigade members as Alverez and Vista were the leaders of the unit. The burden of command weighed heavily upon their shoulders even in prison. A set date for the return of the Miami

Brigade to the United States let off some of the stress Alverez and Vista were feeling.

ROBERT KENNEDY WAS WORKING OUT THE DETAILS FOR THE TRANSFER of the farm equipment to Cuba. Estevez was insistent the United States ship all of the tractors to Havana in a timely manner. As Robert Kennedy had conducted the secret talks he needed to hammer out any problems that arose. A cargo freighter would be heading to Cuba in a matter of hours. Estevez was assured that the tractors were on their way:

"Estevez as promised those tractors are heading to Cuba aboard a cargo freighter. The United States values the deal it has made for the return of the Miami Brigade. Now if you wish to call off the deal I am certain that Castro would be very interested in hearing your side of the story when he got the news." Robert stated.

"No, that is not necessary the deal must proceed and those tractors are too important to abandon the deal. I am willing to be patient. It appears one of our clocks was too fast by several hours. I shall reset the device at once as to prevent further mistakes." Estevez confirmed.

"Excellent, I am glad to hear that everything is still on schedule as any delay is unacceptable on the other end of the deal as well. The Miami Brigade will be returned on December 29 as promised by Cuba or those tractors will be bombed into tiny pieces by our jets. Do I make myself clear Estevez?" Robert inquired.

"Of course, the Miami Brigade will arrive on time as the matter has the personal assurance of Castro. He is a man that keeps his word in such matters." Estevez promised.

"That I am confident of. This deal is in the best interests of our two nations. I want it to work out and so do you thus wait for the tractors and they will be there in Cuba before you know it. I do not wish to hear from you again as these conversations are no longer necessary. You just hold up your end of the deal and all will be fine between our two nations." Robert added.

Having smoothed over the matter, Robert Kennedy hung up the phone not wanting to hear from Estevez ever again for any reason. Delivering the tractors was the first part of the deal with the Miami Brigade being released some 27 days later. Castro had insisted that the tractors arrive first before anyone was released. Wanting to put the deal into full swing Robert Kennedy agreed to this condition of the bargain. He had warned Estevez of what would happen to the tractors if the Miami Brigade was not in Florida on December 29th. This was no idle threat as Robert Kennedy would demand that the tractors were destroyed if the deal fell through.

Estevez tried to appear tough and the effort backfired on him as Robert Kennedy had enough experience to know when he was being bluffed. This shipload of tractors was too valuable to Cuba for Estevez to back out of the deal or threaten the United States. Tensions were still high between Cuba and the United States. It was only normal that both sides distrusted one another. Robert Kennedy was happy to be done with the matter as he had been the point man for the talks with Cuba and reaching a deal that both sides could accept. The entire process had taken a toll on his patience.

President Kennedy was pleased with the deal as it gave his administration closure for the Bay of Pigs Invasion. The matter had hung over the White House for as long as the prisoners were in Havana. Other events had occurred, but the return of the Miami Brigade remained an issue that continued to linger. Reporters always brought up the question whenever it was a slow day at the daily briefing in the White House. With a deal now playing out with Cuba it gave President Kennedy the ability to move on to other problems and challenges. The White House had more on its agenda than dealing with Cuba for the rest of Kennedy's first term.

CASTRO AND CHE INSPECTED THE TRACTORS WHICH HAD BEEN SENT by the United States. All of the vehicles were brand new and could help Cuba with its agriculture. Castro puffed a cigar as he turned to discuss the great deal he had agreed to with the United States:

"These tractors are all together worth 43 million dollars and in exchange all I must give up is the Miami Brigade. It is a deal worthy of song. These machines will help our farming and harvesting and replace old tractors which have been running poorly for years." Castro observed.

"The Kennedy Administration has been made to pay a high price for the release of the Miami Brigade. The image of Cuba has once again been enhanced. Even during the missile crisis our prestige did not suffer as the whole world concerned themselves with the actions of this island nation." Che added.

"I have still emerged on top and that is all that matters. Kennedy may have earned the cameras for a few weeks but my place in history is chiseled in stone. Cuba is a nation that is prospering because of my leadership and soon the countries of South America shall follow in the footsteps of Cuba and begin a revolution. I have spoken once again with the Soviet Union and they are willing to give you support with the revolutions. All they want is to see success and the money will be added to your coffers. I shall miss you. Cuba has benefited from your advice and I have enjoyed your company." Castro remarked.

"In some ways I shall miss Cuba as well. My time here has been well spent. I have learned many things and that is invaluable knowledge." Che stated.

As promised Castro would be letting Che continue on his quest to start revolutions in South American once the month was over. It had been a long time goal that still filled Guevara with passion. Castro was still concerned that President Kennedy might attempt an assassination, but he felt that Cuba would not be touched. The recent events during the Cuban Missile Crisis had forced the United States to make a promise not to invade Cuba. While Castro did not place much stock in the promises of the United States this one had been made publicly once the critical deal with the Soviet Union was reached to remove the nuclear missiles.

The large shipment of tractors that Cuba had received from the United States was another victory for Castro. He had proven once again that Cuba could gain from a deal with the United States. The Miami Brigade would be released, but for a price that made Castro more of a hero in the eyes of his people. Che was happy for both Castro and Cuba. The lure of going to start revolutions in South America however remained strong. Che felt that his contributions to Cuba were becoming less important with each passing month.

Castro and Che had spent years fighting against Batista and several more ruling Cuba, but soon it would be time for them to go their different ways. All of their efforts were already legends as Cuba had been shaped by the two men in more ways than the past several leaders combined. Still Che craved more revolutions and Castro wanted to remain in Cuba to continue with his socialism experiment. The partnership between the two men had transformed Cuba for the better in their eyes. Castro wished his friend well; the Cuban leader was looking forward to seeing Che succeed in starting revolutions South America.

DECEMBER 29, 1962
HAVANA, CUBA,
4:00 AM:

ALVEREZ AND VISTA WERE AWOKEN FROM THEIR SLEEP BY THE SOUND of whistles and megaphones. The Cuban guards were under strict orders to quickly move the men of the Miami Brigade to their departure vehicles. Buses and cargo trucks were waiting outside to transport the unit to the northern coast where a ship would take the brigade to Florida. This was the moment all of the men had prayed for since setting foot inside the prison in April of 1961 over a year and a half earlier. All of the men were lined up for a quick count by the guards before being ordered to march to the buses and cargo trucks parked out in the front of the prison.

Feelings of joy and elation surged through all the men as they walked briskly out of the prison and onto the awaiting vehicles. Alverez and Vista paused to offer a salute to the graves of the 10 officers who had been executed on the orders of Castro. It was a quick gesture and one that some of the other men took part in as well. All of the guards were being pressured to get the men on their way to the harbor as Castro wanted to be done with the Miami Brigade. Once it was quickly verified that all of the men were aboard the vehicles the drives were told to start heading north. Alverez and Vista talked about finally being free from the prison:

"Our day of deliverance has finally come. I did not think that any of us would walk out of that prison. It appears all of us owe the United States a debt of gratitude for their efforts in getting us released." Vista observed.

"We owe more than gratitude; our very lives are owed to the United States as Castro probably wanted us all to be shot as traitors. Whoever talked Cuba into releasing us from prison deserves thanks from the entire brigade. I did not think our freedom would come either, but here we are heading to the United States. It is fitting that once again our journey takes us to Miami. That city is where this unit was formed from. We leave Cuba a second time and our hopes are no longer as bright as they were. Our dreams of revolution and overthrowing Castro have been brought back to the reality to the situation. Cuba is not going to change its government for a very long time. We must all accept this painful truth." Alverez explained.

"I have a feeling that these men are more concerned with their own lives now than revolution. We have survived both a failed invasion and prison. That is not easily done by any man in Cuba. Our freedom is a gift and we must all enjoy it to the fullest in the United States. I for one intend to leave this entire ordeal behind me as best I can. We are civilians once again." Vista commented.

Once again there was a future for the men that walked out of the Havana Prison. The surviving members of the Miami Brigade were on their way to freedom out of a land of tyranny. Alverez and Vista were the only ones to reflect on the past. The rest of the men vowed to put the failed invasion and prison time into their memories as their lives awaited them. The darkness outside reflected the uncertainty about the future. While not depressing the men were unsure about what lay in store and this gave them hope that good times might be among what was to come in the future.

1 HOUR LATER:

THE CONVOY OF VEHICLES STOPPED A FEW HUNDRED FEET SHORT OF A large cargo freighter that was moored at one of the piers. Alverez and Vista stepped off the lead bus as they looked north towards freedom. The men assembled and were soon given the signal to board the freighter. The gangplank was quickly filled by a long stream of men who filed onto the ship. Alverez and Vista were among the last to board the freighter. Off in the distance the sun was beginning to rise. All of the men looked out towards the horizon as it was a sight to behold. During their time in prison the windows were too off the ground to allow for a good view of the rising sun.

Another head count was quickly taken and the captain was told to set sail without delay. All the men began to cheer and sing songs. It was an emotional moment for every member of the Miami Brigade. For many of the men this departure from Cuba was filled with more joy than terror. Fleeing from Batista or Castro had been an ordeal the first time. Now the men were heading towards something positive and away from a terrible past year and a half. Alverez and Vista were filled with mixed emotions about the future. Living in the United States was a blessing in many ways. Miami contained an ever present reminder of Cuba. As people were always more important than land there was hope for the men to have a community of their own people once again. It would be different from Cuba, but the culture and memories were bound to be similar.

Though the men focused on the future they also spent some time reflecting on the Miami Brigade. It had been a big part of their lives for over two and a half years. The bonds of friendship and brotherhood were still strong among the men who fought side by side. Spending a year and a half in prison also forged tight links between the men as adversity brought them together. Survival had been the only goal of the 1,276 surviving members of the Miami Brigade for their time in prison. New goals could now be set by the men as they were civilians once again.

Alverez and Vista were proud to have led the men as it was a challenge which took all their energies.

MIAMI, FL, 2:00 PM:

THE MEN OF THE MIAMI BRIGADE HAD ARRIVED IN FLORIDA WHERE they were greeted by a convoy of buses that would transport them to the Orange Bowl. There a welcome back party was to be thrown in their honor as the final matter in the Bay of Pigs Invasion was put to rest by the United States. Reporters took pictures and began writing stories about the Miami Brigade. This was a big media event as it carried the reminder of the largest blunder in the Kennedy Administration. While many in the American public had forgotten about the men of the Miami Brigade the media did not.

This was a time of remembrance and healing for the men of the Miami Brigade. Ten empty white chairs were setup for the officers who had been executed in prison. Alverez and Vista looked over towards an American flag and smiled. They were back in a nation that allowed all of their basic freedoms to be respect. It was also a subtle reminder of the Cuban flag which also contained the colors red, white and blue. Grateful to be back among a nation that permitted so much freedom the men of the Miami Brigade relished the ability to be looked upon as heroes instead of traitors.

President Kennedy had come in person to meet with the members of the Miami Brigade at the Orange Bowl. The officers and men were given uniforms which they happily traded with their prison clothes to look like soldiers once again. Kennedy came both to honor the brigade and remember those who lost their lives in the Bay of Pigs Invasion. He shook hands with many of the men before heading over to the podium to address to the brigade. The president smiled before beginning his speech as he wanted to place the audience at ease if even just for a few seconds. Then Kennedy began his address and it was delivered with his usual gift for eloquence:

"It is fitting that this reception is taking place in Miami as that is where this brigade came from. Each of you gave a full measure of devotion to the cause of freedom during Operation Zapata. The sacrifice of the men who died shall not be forgotten as they gave their lives to put an end to tyranny. In April of last year this brigade went to Cuba to liberate that nation from Castro. Although the effort failed the bravery and daring of these men must not be forgotten. All of you struggled to fight an enemy several dozen times your size. It was a brief conflict that turned this brigade from another unit into a legend. We are glad to have you back. I ordered the invasion to take place because I believed that Castro was an evil man. That fact is still true. I ordered the invasion because Cuba deserved to live under a democratic government. That also is still true. You men answered the call of duty and fought for what you believed in. That is a noble deed and the United States thanks you for your service to the great cause of freedom. The Miami Brigade shall persist in memory as its time as a military unit has come to an end. Col. Alverez your brigade has fought for freedom and will be awarded a unit citation for valor. These fine men are the bedrock of any civilization. May your lives in the United States be happy and prosperous ones. Welcome back men of the Miami Brigade as you have earned the many freedoms that we take for granted in our daily lives." Kennedy stated.

Col. Alverez shook hands with President Kennedy and then carefully read off a list of the men who died as part of Operation

Zapata. There were five minutes of silence as Alverez went down the list of 124 names. Once all of the names were read a flag of the Miami Brigade was lowered to signal the disbandment of the unit. Tears were shed by some of the men. Others were grateful that their long ordeal was finally over with. Vista spoke with Alverez as the men talked amongst themselves:

"Do you think that Castro will ever be assassinated by the United States?" Vista asked.

"At this point that does not matter. We were there and his support is strong. The people of Cuba are behind the man and that is all that counts. As for the brigade it is now part of history. These men fought for freedom and yet the struggle goes on. Cuba and the United States are both on opposing sides of the matter. Cuba is run by a man who wants total control. The United States is run by many men who want some control. Castro might be gone one day, but until that day arrives we have our own lives to get on with. My time commanding the Miami Brigade was a joyful one. Operation Zapata may have failed, but the spirit of the brigade shall never die. These men will tell the story of how they went to Cuba to free it from a dictator named Castro. Their deeds will live on through tales told to future generations. We took part in history and though the result was not as we desired the acts of the Miami Brigade were still worthwhile. The most one can give is their full measure of devotion. I think the great President Lincoln said something to that effect. Freedom is worth dying for, but the Miami Brigade was not enough to free Cuba. Our true victory comes from living free here in the United States." Alverez answered.

"What will you do now?" Vista inquired.

"I can tell you one thing; I am not going to be driving taxi cabs for the rest of my days." Alverez laughed.

EPILOGUE

From start to finish the Bay of Pigs Invasion had been planned and executed with way too much hope and not enough attention paid to the reality of the situation in Cuba with regards to Castro's power. Mainly the blame falls upon the CIA for poor operational planning, but Eisenhower and Kennedy share some of the fault for their own decisions. The goal of the invasion was noble, but its execution proved to be deeply flawed which cost the lives of men and doomed the entire operation to utter failure after a few days. The following is a breakdown of what went wrong during the Bay of Pigs Invasion:

1.) Too Bold A Plan:

What the CIA had envisioned in 1959 was a plan that sounded like a raid or terrorist tactics. A group of a few hundred Cuban exiles would be sent to Cuba to blow up buildings and cause general chaos. This chaos was in theory supposed to start a revolution against Castro. This plan was scrapped and a new one created that bordered on serious overreach. A force of 1,400 men was going to be trained to invade and spread a revolution in Cuba that would overthrow Castro. These men were not to be US Army or US Marines, but instead Cubans recruited from Miami. The brigade would be shipped to Cuba and begin their revolution with no prior steps to ferment a revolution being taken. The CIA had total control over the plan and refused to heed any advice from the JCS (Joint Chiefs of Staff) about the consequences. While the plan was too bold, there were other factors that came into effect during the invasion that doomed it. One of them was the lack of swift action.

2.) Lack of Swift Action:

PRESIDENT EISENHOWER MADE A CRITICAL DECISION TO DELAY OPERation Zapata until after the Election of 1960. This delay allowed the Cubans to create an armed militia in every major city. This several month delay gave Cuba the time it needed to increase its defenses. Che Guevara had advised Castro to create a militia for Cuba to assist the Cuban Army. These militias were vital in stopping and attacking the invaders. Had the invasion taken place months earlier the militias would not have existed and the progress of the brigade could be reached further into Cuba beyond the beachhead. By April 1961 the Cubans were prepared to counter an invasion force.

President Kennedy assumed office in January of 1961 and gave the order for Operation Zapata to begin within less than two weeks. It would not be until April that the military operation took place. This delay of three and a half additional months gave Cuba more time to get ready for a possible invasion. Had a swift attack taken place immediately upon the completion of the training of the Miami Brigade the results of the operation could have been far more in the invaders favor. Castro was aided by Che Guevara's advice and delays by two president which gave his forces time they needed to prepare.

3.) Lack of Air Superiority:

PRESIDENT KENNEDY COMPOUNDED THE PROBLEMS MADE BY EISENhower when he ordered that only a single set of airstrikes be conducted against Cuba. This limited the number of planes that could be destroyed on the ground. In the end a few Cuban planes managed to avoid being strafed and shot down a large number of the A-26s when the invasion took place. If more airstrikes were allowed the entire Cuban Air Force would have been destroyed instead of just a large portion of it. In the end two Cuban planes wreaked havoc on the invasion force and planes assigned to protect them.

Total air superiority can make the difference between victory and defeat in war. The Cuban Air Force could have been eliminated on the ground. This would have allowed the Miami Brigade to land unopposed and have all of their supplies. In addition the American planes could have stayed longer to provide cover for the men while they were still on the beaches.

4.) Lack of Intelligence:

THE CIA BASED ALL OF ITS PLANS OFF INTELLIGENCE WHICH IT GATHered from informants and its own spies. These sources were not reliable and proved to be unaware of what Castro was really doing. The assumption that the people of Cuba would rise up was wrong, the assumption that a small force of Cubans could start a large scale revolution was wrong. The assumption that the US could remain as a secret force aiding the invaders was wrong. Castro was aware that the United States might attempt a military action of some kind. He took all of the steps required to ensure his regime remained in power.

The intelligence which predicted that Castro could be easily toppled was wrong. All together the CIA proved to be wrong on just about everything except that the Cuban Air Force could be disabled with enough airstrikes. This lack of accurate intelligence led to one mistake after another being made in the planning and execution of Operation Zapata. These mistakes were not trivial and results in the failure of the operation and the loss of 114 lives. The CIA put together a plan that did not take into account the reality of Cuba and how hard it would be to topple Castro. They went ahead with the idea that everything would fall into place. This fantasies were nothing more than wishful by the CIA agents.

5.) Conclusions:

OPERATION ZAPATA WAS A DEEPLY FLAWED PLAN THAT STOOD VIRTU-
ally no chance of succeeding. The CIA had known this fact and
finally in 1997 admitted that its own senior officials knew that
the invasion of Cuba was pure folly. Both President Eisenhower
and President Kennedy made mistakes which compounded the
flawed CIA plan. While bold by design the invasion of Cuba
was too small to achieve any of its objectives. The militias in
Cuba were decisive to defeating the invaders. The people of
Cuba rallied behind Castro instead of joining the invaders. It
was a foreign policy nightmare that led directly to the Cuban
Missile Crisis only a year later in 1962.

The daring plan made by the CIA to remove Castro was
based upon their previous success in Guatemala and this confidence proved unfounded. Cuba was under the tight control of
Castro and his government. They were not going to be easily
overthrown. Playing on fears of the Soviet Union turning Cuba
into a staging ground both Eisenhower and Kennedy approved
of force to be used to remove Castro. Ironically these fears came
to pass and nearly started World War III. Though in 1961 the
Bay of Pigs Invasion proved to be a total failure the Cuban Missile Crisis was a triumph for the USA as it managed to compel
the Soviet Union to back down and remove nuclear missiles
from Cuba.

Kennedy had learned from all of the mistakes of the Bay of
Pigs Invasion by fall of 1962. When nuclear missiles were discovered in Cuba it was clear that a direct threat to the United
States existed. For 13 long days in October of 1962 the world
watched as a drama played out in Cuba with the highest of
stakes. Kennedy showed his skills as a good leader by block-
ading Cuba and managing to get Khrushchev to remove the
nuclear missiles. While plans for an invasion of Cuba were once
again drawn up they were not required. Never again would Cuba
be used as a staging ground for Soviet military power.

Che Guevara was killed by operatives in Argentina working
with the CIA in 1967. Castro would survive until 2016 having
lasted through every president from Eisenhower to Obama. Raul

would take over as leader of Cuba in 2006 and remain in power until 2018 when he vowed not to run for office again. The image of the CIA was somewhat tarnished by the Bay of Pigs Invasion, but it continued on through the Cold War without pausing for a moment to consider its folly. The entire plan to invade Cuba carried the hopes of the US to remove Castro, but in the end proved an exercise in utter futility.

The men of the Miami Brigade were not at fault for the failure of the Bay of Pigs Invasion. They all performed their duties as best a military commander could hope for under the circumstances. The brigade was a force which was under-manned for the task it had been given to carry out in Cuba. Starting a revolution was not possible as the people were loyal to Castro. Defeating the Cuban Army was not possible due to its firepower and manpower when compared with a single brigade of 1,400 men. The Cuban Army was comprised of 32,000 soldiers and the many militias in Cuba totaled 300,000 men. Had the US wanted to eliminate Castro and remove his government an invasion by the US Army and US Marines would have been required.

The CIA neglected basic intelligence on the people of Cuba and Castro. They ignored military common sense and persistently misled both President Eisenhower and President Kennedy. This was the Cold War and under that justification Operation Zapata was launched with a flawed plan and no margin for error. When events went against the invasion force failure was the only outcome that could possible result.

THE END